THE WORLD THAT HAMILTON MADE

"Where'd you get the coins?" the tailor asked suspiciously. "You know about Aaron Burr?"

"What about him?" Ves pretended ignorance.

"He's a traitor," explained the tailor. "Was, I should say. President Hamilton had him tried for treason about eighty years ago, and he fled to Mexico. Hamilton sent the army in to hunt him down. That's how we ended up being at war with Spain and France, and an ally of Great Britain, so soon after fighting the Revolution. The War of 1814, we call it."

"But that was"—Ves did some fast mental arithmetic—"eighty-three years ago. What has that got to do with our loyalty?"

"There is a group of malcontents in this country," the tailor said, "who call themselves Burrites. They want a popular democracy. That sort of thing. You know what it says over the Hamilton Monument: *The People are Turbulent and Changing.* It is not respectable to talk about Aaron Burr . . . and to have a gold coin with Burr's face on it is unpatriotic."

Worse, Ves thought to himself, in this particular alternate America, it was downright dangerous. . . .

THE WHENABOUTS OF BURR

Michael Kurland

DAW BOOKS, INC.

DONALD A. WOLLHEIM, PUBLISHER

1301 Avenue of the Americas
New York, N. Y.   10019

FIRST PRINTING, JULY 1975

1 2 3 4 5 6 7 8 9

PRINTED IN U.S.A.

ONE

||||||||||||||||||||||||||||||||

Professor William Kranzler, perhaps the world's greatest authority on the subject of the Constitution of the United States, was performing a daily and delightful ritual.

"Morning, Professor," said the guard.

"Good morning, Mr. McDowell," said Kranzler, as always. The five years which had elapsed since his retirement as Professor of the History of the American Constitution at the National University had not witnessed any lessening in his attachment to his ritual: on the contrary, it allowed him all the more time to devote to it.

"Good moring, Professor," said the next guard.

"Good morning, Mr. Lundberg."

There was the Shrine, as he always thought of the Exhibition Hall, in which was preserved what Gladstone had called, "the greatest political document to be produced by the hand of man." There it was, *the* document itself: sealed in strong but transparent crystal, filled with preservative helium gas, set and arranged so that at any threat of violence, immediate or otherwise, the entire case containing it would safely sink deep into a sunken vault upon a most ingenious and cleverly-controlled mechanism.

"Good morning, Professor," said the third guard, adding —with permissible familiarity, for he was the longest in service of any of the guards—"Well, it's still here."

"Good morning, Mr. Luisi." Kranzler gave a small, grave smile, stopped, allowed his eyes to rest upon The Document. "Yes, and thank God it still is."

His eyes slowly scanned the pages of beautiful 18th century penmanship. *We, the people of the United States, in order to form* . . . It was still there. All of it. His eyes moved, his mind pondered, his tongue moved voicelessly, his mind savored. The Congress shall have power. A

5

key phrase. Under the Articles of Confederation, the Congress had not had power.

. . . and fix the standards of weights and measures . . .

In 1866 The Congress had allowed the metric system to become optional, but few indeed were those who had picked up the option. Fairly soon now, perhaps within the decade, The Congress would continue the task of making that system compulsory. It would be difficult for a while. No matter. The people of the United States could do without the inch and ounce, as they had—for all practical purposes—been doing without, say, the gill, the ell, the peck and the perch.

What the people of the United States could *not* do without was The Constitution of the United States. This, as an intangible, was the nation's greatest possession. And the nation's most precious tangible possession? Why, what else save this document, the original copy of The Constitution. *The President . . . shall take care . . .*

William Kranzler had a secret wish that some of the customs appropriate to the sacred things of sundry religions might apply to the precious parchment in the sealed case. He should have liked to have pressed his brow or his lips thereunto, genuflected, prostrated himself, held up his hands, removed his shoes, covered his head, or done something or other with the hem of his garments: surely none of these gestures of infinite affection and respect could come under the ban which he saw before his very eyes this very moment to the effect that *no religious test shall ever be required as a qualification to any office or public trust under the United States . . .* surely?

" 'And did these eyes see Franklin plain?' " he asked himself, paraphrasing. Not exactly "these eyes." But these sheets of heavy parchment had. Well . . . not exactly *seen . . .* been touched by. There was old Ben's signature. And those of the others. *Done in convention by the unanimous consent of the States present . . . In witness whereof, we have hereunto subscribed our names.*

His lips moved soundlessly; they could have moved—in fact, they often *did* move—soundlessly, in the dark, repeating the august syllables. *George Washington, President and Deputy from Virginia. New Hampshire: John Langdon, Nicholas Gilman. Massachusetts: Nathaniel Gorham, Rufus King. Connecticut: William Samuel Johnson, Roger Sherman.* Yes, yes, surely as long as this venerable document survived and was well, the United States would survive and be well. *Connecticut: William Samuel Johnson, Roger Sherman. New York: Aaron Burr . . .*

"—Lundberg! McDowell! Get an ambulance! Grab the phone! Professor Kranzler's had a stroke or something!— Hey, Professor. Professor? You all right? Professor?"

Ves Romero was working, rather desultorily, on his collection of Estonian incunabula. There was a certain *éclat* in being the largest private collector of Estonian incunabula, but not much. After all, when you come right down to it, it was not a very large field to collect in. And he had given up trying to exchange information with the Museum of Ethnic Treasures in Tallin, because every time he wrote to them he received back the same form letter; the one beginning *Workers and Peasants of the District of Columbia.* However, it did give him a good excuse to have a locked cabinet. Inside the steel doors, behind the document case, he also kept two derringers, a bottle of Jim Beam, some clean glasses, a bag of potato chips, and a pornographic magazine. Inside the latter was concealed the latest issue of a somewhat smaller publication entitled *Superhero's Pal Zap.*

The combination to the locked cabinet was hidden behind a framed piece of pseudo-parchment which announced that Amerigo Vespucci Romero was a member in good standing of the North American Association of Investigators of Insurance Frauds.

A wall clock very softly went *ping* three times fast, then one time slowly. Ves quickly slid the comic book back inside the porno mag, slipped the latter behind the document case, and closed the safe. Then he got down from the chair and walked over and unlocked the door. Mrs. Montefugoni, his housekeeper, looked at him with disapprobation. "You eat potato chips again," she said. "Come dinner, you push away the green spaghetti, 'Too much starch,' you going to tell me. *Maron!*" Abruptly abandoning this disquisition, "The Commissioner here," she announced. "Straighten up you tie. Have respect. Go."

The old brick house on Zee Street was small, set between its deep lawn and shallow backyard, but since his wife had died and he had retired from business, it often seemed too large for Ves. In the same way, his days, which had once been all too short to accomplish everything,

now often stretched out incalculably long. Several emotions
lighting up his face, square as his body, he stretched out
his hand to the man standing in front of the fireplace.
(Mrs. Montefugoni, a native of Tuscany, where anything
of a date later than Lars Porsena was suspected and con-
demned, had little use for antiquity as understood in the
United States: left to herself she would have bricked up
the fireplace and installed an electric heater.)

"Nate!" Ves exclaimed. "Gee, I'm glad to see you!
Your business is always my pleasure. What brings you
here at this hour?"

Nathan Hale Swift returned the firm handshake. "It's
a long story," he said, perhaps obliquely. Ves, recognizing
the code phrase, turned to his housekeeper who was
hovering in the doorway, smiling respectfully at "the Commissioner," as she—having her own way with titles—insisted on calling him.

"Let's have some of your special coffee, Mrs. M.," he
said.

"You like?" she asked the guest, ignoring her employer.

"That's the chief reason I come here, *Madama*," said
Nate. Beaming transcendentally, the housekeeper withdrew.
First she would roast the beans, then she would grind
them, then she would spice the grind, then—by an arcane
process known to herself and to a small machine the like
of which was procurable nowhere in the United States—
then she would make the coffee. Anyone who unwisely
mentioned the words *instant coffee* to Mrs. Montefugoni
would have suffered her instant displeasure.

As the kitchen door closed behind her, Swift's smile
faded. "This is something very serious, Ves," he said.

"I guessed that. What is it?"

Swift's long and narrow face winced. He shook his head,
not negatively, but in perplexity.

"The Constitution of the United States has been stolen,"
he said.

There was a silence in the warm, quiet room. Then, "I
don't quite—" Ves was beginning.

"I mean, the original document of the final draft of the
Constitution, as signed by the delegates to the Constitutional Convention in Philadelphia in 1789, has been stolen
from the National Archives Exhibition Hall." Abruptly,
Swift folded his long legs and sat down.

Ves's mouth moved a moment before he spoke. "But that's terrible," he said. "*Who*—?"

Again Swift shook his head. "No idea. Nobody has any idea. I mean—"

"But didn't the guards *see?*"

"Nobody saw."

Ves blinked. "Now, come on now, Nate," he said. "I've *been* there. The Constitution, the Declaration of Independence, and the Bill of Rights, why, they're guarded day and night, and they're sealed in bronze cases. It's impossible."

Nate nodded, ran a long, lean hand over his dark hair. "I quite agree. It *is* impossible. Still, that's what happened . . ." He went on to explain that the theft had been first noticed by Professor William Kranzler, the famed expert on the history of the Constitution, shortly after ten o'clock that morning. The shock had resulted in the older man's fainting dead away; on his recovery—fortunately, without any injuries or physical aftereffects—he had at once reported the matter to Dr. Stenberry, the National Archivist, who immediately came to see for himself and immediately ordered the Exhibition Hall closed to the public "for repairs."

"Stenberry notified the President's Secretary, the Secretary notified the President and the President called me," Nat said, meanwhile opening his briefcase and removing a sheet of paper.

"And here you are," Ves said. "As always, I am flattered. In this case, well, I feel like Abe Lincoln's story of the man who was ridden out of town on a rail: 'if it wasn't for the honor of the thing, I'd sooner walk' . . . What is the Xerox?"

Swift passed it over. "This is what, I mean, this is a copy of what is now in, or, damn it, my tongue won't stay clear of my teeth!" He paused, took several slow breaths, continued, "This is a xerox copy of the document which Professor Kranzler discovered had been substituted for the original copy of the Constitution. It took them two and a half hours to open the case in order to get at the substitute."

Ves Romero took the glossy sheet and had begun to read it very slowly, starting with the Preamble; Nate, impatiently, pointed to a particular line near the end of the document. Ves read that one quickly enough, grunted, smiled quickly, crookedly, said: "I suppose I ought to be ashamed, but—well, I didn't realize that Aaron Burr *had* signed the Constitution for New York State—"

Nate's thin face was briefly crossed by an even thinner smile. "He didn't sign it. Not for New York State nor for any other state. Do you know who *did* sign for New York State?" His friend's head swung slowly into a blank shake. "Okay. Neither did I remember. Well, it's not exactly classified information.

"The delegate who signed the United States Constitution on behalf of New York State was Alexander Hamilton."

At the mention of this familiar name, Ves Romero's face cleared . . . was again clouded with a frown . . . suddenly began to do funny little things with itself. "Hey," said Amerigo Vespucci Romero. "Oh," he said. "But," he said. "Alexander Hamilton. He was, oh, he was the first Secretary of the Navy. I mean, the *Treasury*. He said, 'Your People, sir, is a great Beast.' He was, uh, uh, he was shot. Yeah! He was in a duel. He was killed. He was—"

Nate nodded grimly, wearily. "Yes. In Weehawken, New Jersey. On July 11, 1804. And the man who fired the fatal shot was—"

Ves's memory finally came through, like money spilling out of a jackpot. "Aaron Burr!" he cried. *"Aaron Burr!"*

The Constitution of the United States makes no mention of an F.B.I. It does not, for that matter, mention a Secret Service. Or a Flag, or a National Anthem, or—but we digress. It does, however, state, and state quite plainly, that *The Congress shall have power to fix the standards of weights and measures;* accordingly a Bureau of Weights and Measures was by Act of Congress set up in 1801: henceforth, a pound in Richmond, Virginia was a pound in Richmond, N.Y.; and a yard of cloth spun in Salem, Massachusetts measured a yard when purchased in Salem, South Carolina. That the utility of this office went without saying, goes without saying. Federalists and Whigs, Republican-Democrats, Populists and Greenbackers, Barn-burners and Locofocos, Dixiecrats and Socialists, all observed towards the Bureau of Weights and Measures a strictly hands-off policy. That is, they did not exactly observe it.

They never even thought about it.

Time passes. In 1996, the voters (including for the first

time those of the new states of Guam and the Virgin
Islands) swept into presidential office that darkest of dark
horses, Rep. Victor Gosport (Dem., Idaho), the youngest
ever to hold that office—perhaps because they really
wanted a Democrat in the White House. Perhaps because
Luella (Mrs. Victor) Gosport, one week before election
day, was safely delivered of triplets: all boys. Or, perhaps
because certain aspects of the Democratic candidate's
campaign had been, with uncanny scientific accuracy,
masterminded by the candidate's friend, Dr. Dunstan Dutton.

Dunstan Dutton (Ph.D., Ph.D., D.Sc., D.Phil.), having
collected the figures on the order and location of every
appearance made by every presidential candidate over the
past fifty years, as well as sundry other statistics, by a
process understood only by himself and one selfless assis-
tant, correlated them all and drew up the most baffling
campaign schedule in American history. Andrew Johnson
had "swung around the circle," Major William McKinley
had sat on his front porch. Harry Truman got off the train
at whistle-stops, or sometimes spoke from the end of the
train without getting off . . .

Victor Gosport sometimes zigged and sometimes zagged;
one day he spoke at a county fair in Delaware and the
next he showed up at a high school in Lubbock, Texas;
thence to the Methodist Home for the Aged in Skaneateles,
next at Pershing Square; from there by helicopter to
Orange County, till that moment an enemy stronghold—

Students of political scenes were baffled. Maybe Victor
Gosport was, too. But he had faith in Dr. Dunstan Dutton. It was not Money which had brought this unassuming
man to the service of the Democratic candidate, nor a desire to be a kingmaker, although he did (when pressed)
describe himself as a "philosophical Democrat." He did
not even develop the winning strategy (if indeed it was
the strategy which won the election, and not Luella and
the triplets) for the pleasure of seeing if it would succeed.
Dutton was motivated purely and simply by a political
ambition, and his political ambition was a pure and simple
one, indeed.

He wanted to be the Director of the Bureau of Weights
and Measures. It was so arranged.

President Gosport was not a particularly deep and
devious man; if anything, he was indeed too open and

disingenuous for his own, and perhaps the country's, good. There was, however, one streak of cunning which was basic to his very nature, and it was this: *he did not trust the F.B.I. and he took steps to act behind its collective back.*

"They all hate the President—whoever he is," he said.

He said it quietly, and under circumstances which assured him that he was not going to be overheard or bugged. He said it to his college roommate, Nathan Hale (Nate) Swift, formerly of U.S.C.G.C.S.I. Det. L, more commonly known as Coast Guard Intelligence. "I wouldn't trust them pricks anymore than I could throw them," he added, moodily, discussing his problem with Nate, while gloomily tugging his beard (he was the first bearded president since Benjamin Harrison). "I tell them I want something done—*me*, mind you: President of the United *Stat*es—and that dumb prick Nephi Gundarson, I mean, J. Edgar was bad enough, but this *new* prick, wow! He says, 'Well, we'll do what we can, Mr. President,' the prick. Then he either leaks it to the goddamn press, or else, would you believe it, Nate? *Nothing happens!*"

"The pricks," said Nate, sympathetically.

The President meditated, a scowl upon his wholesome, craggy features. "Abe Lincoln never had these problems", he said, after a while. "He wanted a man followed, or something, he just said to Alan Pinkerton, 'Follow that man!' And old Pinkerton just said, uh, 'Yes, Mr. President!' And that was *that. My* Secret Service, they couldn't follow an elephant's tracks in the snow, unless it had counterfeit money up its trunk . . ." His voice ebbed away, and again he tugged his beard.

Nate made a sympathetic sound. After a minute he asked, "But . . . Vic . . . what about all the Defense Department intelligence groups and the C.I.A. and, mmm, the . . . mmm . . ."

But all of these groups were diffuse, hierarchical; it was impossible to ask that a confidential mission be carried out by any of them on behalf of the President and remain confidential. "Either the guy is so low on the totem pole that a million guys above him have to know what he's doing, or he's so high on the totem pole that he can't possibly do it himself. If I say, 'Follow that man!', it goes down on 8700 hunks of paper, it goes down on magnetic tape, it goes down on computer tape, it goes down on ticker tape and before you can *blink,* more people know about it than Carter has liver pills. By *that* time, the man I might have wanted to be followed is in Rio de Janeiro or some place, swinging it up."

Nate said, softly, "I begin to see the problem, Vic."

"Call me Mr. President," the President said, absent-mindedly. And he went on to say that he could not assign members of his personal White House staff to any of these confidential tasks, because they were all known. Suppose the press were to ask, "Why was Presidential Aide Flanders Krum seen in Omaha last Tuesday, following a man?" How would it look? Congress would have its attention diverted and if there was one thing which the President did not want in such matters, it was to divert the attention of Congress.

Although the people of the United States had elected a Democratic president, it (or they) had not elected a Democratic congress. A Republican congress had not exactly been elected, either; in fact, the balance of power was precariously being held by a trio of mavericks, "Two FOTs and a Freebi," as Victor Gosport called them. One district in Vermont and one district in Texas had turned out their incumbents in favor of the candidates of the Fine Old (American) Traditions Party, whose platform included the designation of blueberry pie as the National Dish, and the abolition of federal income tax; while the solidly prosperous, mostly Caucasian, Silk Stocking District of Manhattan's Upper East Side had chosen to be represented in Washington by a candidate of the Free Black Independent Party, evidently thrilled by his promise to cut all their throats at the first opportunity.

"I've got a legislative program to get through Congress," the President said. "I promised the American People. So I got to be careful that Congress doesn't get side-tracked by diversionary tactics, Nate. The F.B.I. and the other big Snoop Sections, they're all a bunch of spies, the pricks. Just love to embarrass me by leaking confidential info. And then what can I do about it? Nothing. No. I cannot trust them. I can trust *you,* Nate. Known you for years. Also, you were in Coast Guard Intelligence, one of the nation's top spook outfits. If I say to you, 'follow that man', why, you are by God going to *follow* that man. Yourself, without letting the whole goddamn world know all about it, such as House Republican Leader Winthrop

Scrannel and F.B.I. Director Nephi Gundarson, the pricks."

They were speaking in a White House chamber the existence of which was unknown to the public; in it were such items as a parlor suite left behind by Mrs. Heber Votaw, President Harding's sister; God's own number of moldering trophies shot by Col. Roosevelt; Christmas presents which had met with the disapprobation of First Ladies Hayes, Garfield, Wilson, Hoover, and Truman; and five divans inlaid with mother-in-law-of-pearl and presented by an ousted claimant to one of the Trucial Sheikdoms during the Coolidge Administration. This was known as the Clutter Room, and Luella Gosport had obtained the key from the White House's Housekeeper on a pretext. President Gosport felt confident that it was not bugged.

Nate Swift ran his lean hand over his dark hair. "Mr. President," he said, "I am willing to be of whatever service I can to you, both as an old American and a loyal friend—I mean, as a loyal American and an old friend."

"I'm going to give you a note to Dr. Dutton, the new Director of the Bureau of Weights and Measures," the President decided. "He's going to make you Field Observer."

Swift, who had been leaning back, sat up straighter. The inlaid divan had been designed for shorter, softer bodies than his own. "The Bureau of Weights and *Meas*ures? *Field* Observer?"

The President smiled, pleased both at the thought of his idea and at his friend's reaction to it, which was puzzlement. "That's right. Principle of the Purloined Letter. You want to hide something, leave it laying right out in the open. It'll never be observed. Now, Nephi Gundarson may be a dumb prick, but he's after all not a hundred percent dumb. He'll be watching like a hawk to see what new appointees are going in what slots. But he hasn't got all the time in the world, so of course he'll concentrate on spook sections such as the C.I.A., N.S.A., D.D.I., and *so* on. Will he even *think* of looking into the Bureau of Weights and Measures? Will anybody? Of course not! That's what they call in Hollywood 'the beauty part of it', you see.

"*No*body suspects the Bureau of Weights and Measures! And your title, Field Observer, well, that puts nobody up tight. Investigator, yes. Observer, no. You go anywhere

—anywhere I send you, that is—and you look at anything and you report back to me. That is, of course, you
can make some routine report for the archives of the
Bureau, but that's all. Nobody will bother about it. F.B.I.
has its informants planted all over the place, but not
there!"

He got up, rubbing the base of his spine. "Think of it
this way, Nate. What you'll be doing, you'll be helping
to insure domestic tranquility and promote the general
welfare. You'll take it, of course."

They walked towards the door. "Of course, Mr. President," said Nathan Hale (Nate) Swift.

The late Mr. Romeo Romero, an importer of the finer
sorts of olive oil, antipasto, and tomato conserves, was
proud of his Italian birth and his American citizenship:
therefore he named his first-born son Amerigo Vespucci.
His son was equally proud of both estates, and did not
really disparage his own name. But noting that untutored
American tongues often found it difficult to master all
the syallables of it, soon came to call himself what most of
his friends called him: to wit, simply *Ves*. The firm
of Romero Associates was second to none in the field
of insurance investigations, ranging from checking on
applicants to looking into claims; arson, the firm did
not care to handle, leaving it to well-known specialists
in the field; but for all matters involving the oddly-named
area of "inland marine" policies, the name of Romero
was a byword, and this was hardly less so in cases of
personal liability claims.

The nature of his work, the quickness of his mind,
his natural zeal and indefatigability, resulted in his meeting not only the professional criminals, but magnates and
their wives, stars of stage and screen, foreign nobility,
men and women in every walk (or crouch) of life; he
became aware, almost by second nature, of the little signs
which most of us leave unnoticed, by which the crook so
often gives himself away.

"I go into the office of the firm reporting the losses,"
he explained once to Nate, over a caffè espresso at the
Downtown Chess Club, "and my first question, well, it
might be, 'Who's been taking taxicabs who didn't used to?'
Be surprised, Mr. Swift,"—it was not yet "Nate"—"You'd
be surprised how many embezzlers, they never *think* of

giving themselves away by, say, wearing the fancy clothes to work which they might have bought with their ill-gotten gains, yet somehow they just can't resist calling that taxicab once they leave the office."

Nate looked up from the dissolving heap of cinnamon-sprinkled whipped cream atop the bitter liquid. "And then what?"

Romero shrugged. "Oh, I simply walk up to him and I say, 'The firm is aware that somebody has abused its confidence to the tune of $17,000—or however much the firm has lost, and you'd be surprised how many of them aren't sure exactly what the figure is—but it would rather not prosecute if this can be avoided.' Nine times out of ten, they come clean." He shrugged, sighed. "But . . . you know . . . nine times out of ten, it just got to be *boring*."

His eyes glistened. "And then . . . then, five years back, it will be five years the 11th of April, my dear wife passed away. And after that, well, the taste just seemed to go out of almost everything . . ."

And it was not long after this great loss that Mr. Romero's son and daughter both married. It happened that both his son and his son-in-law were attached to the firm of Romero Associates, and got along well together. Romero the elder called them to him, and said, "Roger, Robert. Take over the business. You know more than I did at your age because you have had educational advantages which I didn't; also here you have a ready-made business, which I didn't; plus you have the old man to advise you when you get into trouble, which I didn't. This way you'll be able to keep the family together, provide for the children which you will have, with God's blessing, and bring them up well. Since Mom died, I don't know, somehow I can't keep my mind on the business the way I used to. Besides, I'm getting on in years and I deserve a little rest. Neither do I believe in keeping children tied to their elders' apron-strings, so to speak, male or female, the way some parents do. Look at Queen Victoria, for example, who should have abdicated years before she died, the way Queen Wilhelmina did, turned the country over to her son and daughter, or however it was; sensible woman."

Also, he said to his son and his son-in-law, "Just pay me a small salary as Consultant, so you can justifiably keep my name on the letterhead, and a percentage of the gross. —That way," he now ceased speaking in retrospect and directed his comments entirely to Nate Swift; "That way, they don't get the idea that they're getting something for nothing, which in my opinion can corrupt young people quickly. So now everybody is happy," he said with a sigh, "and I have no reason in the world to feel the least bit unhappy, which to tell you the truth, I do. Nonetheless." And he sighed once again.

From such a chance meeting over the chessboard and coffee sprang that most unlikely and yet fruitful partnership which, on behalf (though clandestinely, yet honorably) of the President and, through him, the People of the United States, was to solve such matters as the affairs of the knifegrinder and the abbreviated state senator, the case of the foreign agent and the Jersey City pom-pom girl, the mixed-up matter of how the Armenian Ambassador was disentangled from the tuna net in San Pedro Harbor, and—to name but one more—the truly horrifying affair of Rev. Elmo Smith of Omaha (Nebraska) and the twenty-five piranha fish in the swimming pool of the Mayflower Hotel—stories for which the world is not yet prepared—

—and was now to be faced with the greatest challenge yet: to find the missing original parchment of the Constitution of the United States. And to return it . . . unharmed.

TWO

||||||||||||||||||||||||||||

"It doesn't," Amerigo Vespucci Romero said for what must have been the sixtenth time, "make any sense. I mean, forget about the fact that there's no way in the knowledge of the Human Race that such a replacement could have been accomplished; there is—and this is more important —no motive for anyone to have accomplished such a replacement. Motive is the thing, you know. There are all sorts of motives: greed, lust, fear, ambition, religious or philosophical fanaticism, hunger, rivalry, loyalty, anger, and a couple of instinctive reactions. I forgot whether it's fashionable right now to admit that Homo sapiens is possessed of instincts." He was pacing back and forth in his study waving his hand—the one not holding the coffee cup—emphatically at Nathan as he spoke.

"I have a thought on that," Nathan Hale Swift said, balancing his coffee cup on his knee and staring into the fire. "An idea, you might say. It reminds me of something."

"Hah?" Romero asked, stopping in mid-wave.

"It reminds me of something. Of college, actually."

"How's that?"

"Well, you see . . . You know, the President and I were roommates in college . . ."

"You told me, maybe twenty-five times. *He* told me once, I remember."

"Yeah. Well, in college we used to do things like that. I don't mean me, particularly; although I remember once or twice—there was the bell that kept ringing fourteen, and the bulldozer on the third floor of the ad-"

"Nate, what in hell are you talking about? I mean, if you don't mind my asking!"

"Practical jokes. College pranks. That's what this seems like to me, some kind of prank. What else?"

Ves shook his head. "The 'what else' I agree with," he said. "I would like to figure out what else. I admit I'm not up on my college pranks, but is someone—student or no—going to commit an impossible crime merely as a *joke?*"

"That's the point! That's the favorite kind. Like bricking over the end of a hall so that two rooms seem to disappear; or having a bulldozer suddenly appear in the third floor hall of the administration building; or making a four-ton bronze statue of the founder vanish from its pedestal in the middle of the night, leaving an equally massive nude couple in an—ah—embarrassing position in its place. That sort of thing."

"*You* did that?" Ves asked, the astonishment evident in his voice.

"Youth," Swift said apologetically.

"I never thought you had enough imagination," Ves said. "But how does this help us to locate the Constitution?"

"I don't know," Nate admitted. "But I can't think of anything else. I mean, look at it: someone broke into a constantly-guarded room, somehow without being seen, removed a document from a bronze, crystal-faced case— without, incidentally, disturbing the helium atmosphere— and replaced it with an identical document, of the same age, differing only in one signature. It's—"

"Same age?" Ves broke in to ask. "Same age? You mean, the phony, the replacement, is also two hundred and twenty—what?—six years old?"

"I didn't tell you? I guess not. Yeah. The paper is that old. Ink is the right composition and carbon-dates to the same age, plus or minus twenty percent. And the thing is written by hand, not photocopied; and, as best as our experts can tell, it's not a forgery."

"What do you mean, it's not a forgery?" Ves demanded. "What is it then, if it's not a forgery? How can it be . . . Hello, Mrs. Montefugoni. Come in, come in."

"New pot of coffee," Mrs. Montefugoni said, bearing the tray before her as proudly as her eight-year-old self had borne the statue of the sacred lamb on feast day in the procession through the narrow streets of her native village. "And *tartes* for the Commissioner. The cream-fill ones, like he likes." She set the tray down on the coffee table and replaced the empty silver coffeepot with the full silver coffeepot. "And your mail," she added, indicating a clutch of envelopes on one side of the tray.

"Mail," Romero repeated distractedly, picking up the envelopes and staring down at them. "Mail. Mrs. Montefugoni, why do you do this? I have asked you several times not to do this, but iI can't seem to convince you. It isn't right, Mrs. Montefugoni. It is *my* mail, after all."

Swift looked at his friend intently, trying to figure out what he was talking about. Mrs. Montefugoni didn't look embarrassed, ashamed, frightened, or hurt; merely stubborn. "I told you," she said. "Many times. It is for my sister's boy, Vincenti Gerabaldi. He is a collector. Only nine years old, you understand. And you get so many letters from foreign places—and you do not yourself collect . . ."

Then Nate noticed that the upper right hand corners of three of the envelopes had been neatly cut off. "Stamps!" he said.

"*Si,*" Mrs. Montefugoni said. "*Si.* He collect the stamps. And he is very serious, you know. He soak the stamps in some special thing to take them off the paper. And he does not paste them in the, you know, album. At first, when he first get the album, he pasted the stamps in over their pictures—you know they have these little pictures in the book, the album—with white paste. Then he find out he was wrong. Now he uses these tweezers and these little gummy things to stick them in the book. He is very serious."

"A collector!" Nate said, a gleam in his eye.

"But couldn't you wait until I open the letters, *then* rip the stamps off?" Ves complained.

"That must be it!" Nate said, slapping the table.

"What you mean, 'rip'," Mrs. Montefugoni demanded. "I cut neat with scissors. You rip open letter, destroy stamp."

Nate poured a fresh cup of coffee and leaned back, gloating. "Of course! Who else?"

"They're *my* letters," Ves said, weakly fighting a rearguard action.

"Document collector?" Nate wondered aloud. "Autograph collector?"

"Stamp collector," Ves explained. "A nine-year-old stamp collector. Mrs. Montefugoni, perhaps we could reach a compromise. Listen: I promise to open the envelopes carefully and save the stamps for your sister's boy if you will only, please, bring me my mail in its pristine, uncut form."

"No, the Constitution, Ves. That must be it! A collector! A Goddam—excuse me, Mrs. Montefugoni—collector."

"No need to use the bad language," Mrs. Montefugoni said, raising her head to a martyric angle. "You no want me to cut off stamps—ever so neat with snips like I do —then I not evermore cut them off. You rip off envelopes like you want. I find some substitute perversion for my sister's boy Vincenti Gerabaldi." She left the room with a full head of steam.

"She'll pout for days, now that she has an excuse," Romero said. "I'll end up having to raise her salary. Try to stay, if not pure of heart, at least clean of mouth in Mrs. Montefugoni's presence, Nate. You'll end up costing me money. A collector, hah?"

"What else?"

"That's debatable logic."

"Nonsense, it's the best logic in the world. 'When you

have eliminated the impossible, whatever is left, no matter how improbable, must be true.' Sherlock Holmes said that. Something like it, anyway."

"But you haven't eliminated anything. All you've done is come up with a label for the thief, and a possible motive. Still nothing about how this impossible crime was accomplished."

"Well," Swift insisted, "it gives us a direction in which to look, anyway, and that's progress."

"What did you mean before, it's not a forgery?" Romero asked. "How can the substitute be not a forgery—not be a—you know—I think I've been around Mrs. Montefugoni too long. Just because the paper and ink are roughly as old as the original Constitution should be, doesn't mean that it's not a forgery. We could have a careful, clever forger. Or, contrariwise, it could be an ancient forgery. That thing might have been sitting somewhere for two hundred years waiting for someone to pull this practical joke."

"The signatures are real, Ves. At least as far as our experts can tell." Nate Swift spoke slowly and calmly, as though he were relaying quite ordinary information.

"Identical with the ones on the original?"

"No. As you know, no two real signatures are identical. There's always a variance in the way anyone signs his name. Well, these are *not* identical with the original, but are in every case consistent with the way the man signed his name at that period of his life to a degree which, the experts assure us, no human could have duplicated so consistently."

"Even the Burr signature?"

"Even. Isn't it a hell of a thing? You know, if word of this gets out to the public, there'll be rioting in the streets. Particularly in the universities. They haven't had a good excuse to riot in the universities for the past ten years, and they're getting restless for lack of exercise."

"Computers," Romero said firmly.

"Don't be silly, Ves. Everytime anything happens that you don't like or disapprove of, you blame it on computers."

"Sure, look here: you say *they* say that no human could have duplicated the signatures. Nonetheless they *were* duplicated. By your logic, I have eliminated the impossible and computers are left."

"You haven't eliminated anything," Nate told him. "You've only added one to the list."

"List?"

"Last night, before I was authorized to come over here and get your help, we kicked the problem around and made up a list of possible solutions."

"We?"

"Yes. You know: me, and the President, the Secretary of State, the Secretary of the Interior, and the Director of the Bureau of Weights and Measures."

"Quite a kaffeeklatsch," Romero said. "What did you decide?"

"I don't think 'decide' is quite the right word," Swift told him. "The Secretary of State thinks it's Chinese submarines."

"Chinese . . . ?"

". . . Submarines. Yes."

"How—"

"He never said. The Secretary of the Interior has decided that it's the Brotherhood of the Rosy Cross. They're the ones who possess the Secret Power."

"What secret power?"

"They've never said. I suppose if they did, it wouldn't be secret."

"Who does the President think did it?"

"The Republicans."

"Of course. Any other theories?"

"People from the far future, who came back to this time period to rescue the Constitution from an imminent disaster."

"Hm. You know, that one has merit. At least we don't know that it's impossible. Whose idea?"

"The President's twelve-year-old daughter, Emily."

"Well, at least we'll soon know if it's true."

"How's that?"

"We merely await the cataclysm. Meanwhile, as we wait, anything else?"

"Nothing as useful as that batch."

"What about your immediate superior, Dr. Dutton?"

"He tends to think it's the Republicans, except that he allows for the possibility that it's Democrats out to get him. He also mentioned the Vice President."

"The Vice President. The Vice . . ."

"He pointed out that Aaron Burr was once Vice President. You must understand that Dr. Dunstan Dutton is a firm believer in the Great Cypher. He believes that no one can write a document without incrypting his name, address, political philosophy, and waist measurements into the text. He has already proven by cryptology that *King Lear* was written by Isaac Asimov and the Pentateuch was written by Avram Davidson. Dr. Dutton believes in simultaneous creation. Don't ask me, because I don't know."

"Nate, I fear we'll have to leave the administration out of our planning. I don't, somehow, feel that they'll be of any great assistance.

Swift put down his coffee cup and squared his shoulders. "Then it's just you and I," he said. "We two against the Unknown Enemy!"

Ves Romero stared at him. "Nate," he said, "sometimes you frighten me."

"Ah, Ves," Nate said, staring at the wall sadly. "I am the last of the Romantics, and no one understands me any more. Like the dinosaurs, I have outlived my time. I'm a relic of a dead and distant past."

"I haven't seen many disosaurs around recently," Ves said. "And besides, you're only half my age. Maybe a few years more. I have no idea what you're talking about. Also, I have no idea what you think you're talking about. What *are* you talking about?"

"No matter," Nate said. "No matter. Ah, Cyrano, I salute you!" He drew an imaginary sword and pressed it against his nose. Quietly, barely audibly, he began to hum the *Marseillaise*.

Ves pulled a pad of paper toward himself and took a felt tip pen from his shirt pocket. "Let us," he suggested, tapping the pen on the palm of his hand, "analyze the imponderables. Let us list the impossibilities, and see if we can get a clear idea of just what it is that we have to solve."

"Very well," Nate said, pouring himself another cup of Mrs. Montefugoni's special coffee, "list away. I love lists."

"First of all," Ves began, "there's the theft and replacement. Clearly impossible, as it was done without breaking the seals or violating the helium atmosphere."

"A good beginning," Nate said.

"Then there's the document itself—the new document,

that is. A forgery so good that the experts can't tell, except for the self-evident fact that it has to be a forgery."

"Why?" Swift asked.

"What?"

"Why? Why does it have to be a forgery? What if it is a real document? Suppose there were two copies, and Aaron Burr signed the first. Then, for some reason, Alexander Hamilton signed the second and the first disappeared."

"Should be able to check that," Ves said. "Let's see . . ." He went over to his wall of books and browsed amid the history section, pulling out and leafing through a variety of books before settling on three to use. He went back and forth among them, making rapid notes. "Yup," he said finally. "No doubt."

"What?"

"During the Constitutional Convention, which took place in Philadelphia in May and June of 1787, Aaron Burr was a practicing attorney in New York City: Manhattan, to be precise. He had several cases that came to trial at that time. Philadelphia and New York are about ninety miles apart. That's about two-three days by coach, I think. It would mean an absence of at least a week. Burr just wasn't absent from New York for a week. Hamilton was the delegate from New York. Hamilton and Burr were, ah, not the best of friends, even then."

"Well," Nate said stubbornly, "I still say that if our experts have found the replacement Constitution isn't a forgery, then it isn't a forgery."

"I'm familiar with the game of 'our experts are better than your experts,' " Ves said. "As a practicing private detective, I've played it in court many times. But isn't this more a case of 'our experts' versus the laws of logic?"

Nate shook his head. "There are more things under Heaven and Earth, I'm afraid, Amerigo Vespucci, than are allowed for under your laws of logic."

Ves shrugged. "We'll see. I think we'll start with your idea."

"That's fine," Nate agreed. "What idea?"

"The idea that, whatever was done, it was done by a collector. Let's ask around and find out if anyone has expressed an interest in collecting the Constitution."

"You know, when you say it that way," Nate said, "it sounds like a nutty thing to do."

"We'll try it anyway," Ves said. "You know, rare book dealers, autograph places, museums, galleries, auction houses, like that. Someone was interested enough in the Constitution to steal it; maybe he expressed that interest to someone who'll remember."

"Sure," Nate agreed. "We'll go around asking dealers whether anyone's made them an offer for the Constitution recently. You know—the one in Washington under glass."

Ves shrugged. "Worth a try."

THREE

||||||||||||||||||||||||||||

At the seventh place they tried, they struck gold: Brown, Lupoff & Gilden, est. 1868: Rare Books, Manuscripts, Autographs, Coins, Stamps, and Personal Items of the Great, Important, Famous, Notorious, or Noteworthy, Bought & Sold; Appraisals Free; No Estate Too Small.

Mr. Gilden himself helped them. A small man, thin and nervous-looking, with a dark moustache borrowed from a miniature walrus. He was, he assured them from behind the small dealer's table, the fourth of that name in the firm. "My father, his father, and his uncle. The firm was originally called merely 'Brown's', you know. Of course, it was a coffee shop then. Lupoff and Gilden used to meet there every second Sunday and hold an informal rare book and document auction. Gradually, the auctions became more important than the coffee. It's in memory of this tradition that we always keep a pot of coffee brewing for our customers."

"What a nice tradition," Nate said. "I'd like some coffee."

"It's fifty cents a cup," Mr. Gilden told them.

Ves pulled a dollar from his pocket. "My treat," he said. "Could we get some information from you, Mr. Gilden?"

"That's what I'm here for," Gilden said. "One second!" He went off to a corner behind the long counter, and returned with three cups of coffee. "Now, what can I do for you? Cream or sugar?"

"Cream."

"Black."

"Good, here."

"Mr. Gilden, what we'd like to know is: has anyone approached you—your firm—with any unusual requests recently?"

"That's my business, unusual requests," Mr. Gilden told them. "A man wants a note from Dolly Madison to the White House butcher, and is willing to pay five hundred dollars: this isn't an unusual request? Another man, he couldn't care less about Dolly Madison, but a playbill autographed by Harry Lauder will drag a check of four figures out of his wallet. Usual? Collectors—big money collectors—go for the unique, the unusual. They're all specialists."

"It's a certain kind of specialist we're looking for, Mr. Gilden," Nate said. "Has anyone offered to buy anything from you that you, ah, shouldn't be expected to have?"

"Like a government document, for example?" Ves added.

"*I* know what you mean," Mr. Gilden said, his eyes wide. "Spies! Someone must be trying to pass secret information out of the country disguised as an autographed letter—or concealed in the binding of a first edition; I'll bet that's it!"

"Not exactly, Mr. Gilden," Swift said.

"That's good thinking, though," Ves encouraged. "But we're looking for someone who might be making really odd requests. Either buying or selling. Something you just wouldn't expect them to have."

"I see what you mean," Mr. Gilden said, shaking his head rhythmically up and down. "Yes. Wait here a minute, I have something to show you." He trotted off toward the vault at the back of the showroom.

"Aha!" Ves said. "What do you suppose?"

"It couldn't be—" Nate said. Then he shook his head a bit sadly. "No, I suppose not. That would be a bit much."

"I'm sure we're not going to find the, ah, document itself, Nate," Ves told him softly. "Some clue, some trace, some starting point; that's the best we can hope for, and it should be enough for us."

"All kinds of nuts in this business," Mr. Gilden said, coming back to the little table with a small, flat box, looking like a cigar box built to hold one layer of cigars. "Mind you, these aren't for sale." He opened the box and removed several gold coins, which he spread out on the felt top of the table for display. On the face of each coin was an arrogant, strong-nosed, self-willed head, in profile, surrounded by the legend AARON BURR IMP. MEXICO. On the reverse was the device of an eagle on a cactus clutching a snake; on top the words UN EAGLE D'OR. Underneath was the motto: *Don't Tread on Me,* and the date: 1827.

"The things people do," Mr. Gilden said, holding one of the coins between thumb and forefinger and examining it closely. "The workmanship someone put into this, it's incredible. Aaron Burr was never emperor of Mexico, you know."

"I know, it was Hamilton," Nate couldn't help saying.

"Maximilian," Mr. Gilden said, not seeming to notice. "I looked it up. The things people will do for a joke, or a hoax. Incredible. These are mint-quality coins. Really first rate."

"Where did you get them?" Swift asked.

"I bought them. For their weight in gold, you understand. But they're so fine, I'm not going to melt them down. Twenty of them.

"The Federal Bureau of Weights and Measures is going to borrow three," Swift told him, pulling his identification card holder from his jacket pocket. "You'll get a receipt of course, and we'll have them back to you undamaged in about a week."

"I've heard that before," Mr. Gilden said, snatching up the coins. "That's one of the oldest tricks in the books."

It took a half hour to straighten that one out, to convince Brown, Lupoff & most particularly Gilden to entrust three of the coins to a representative of the Federal Government. Nate and Ves returned in high humor to Nate's office in the ancient building that housed the Observational Branch of the Bureau of Weights and Measures.

"Phone call," Swift's secretary declared firmly as they entered the office. She was holding the handpiece at arm's length and facing away from her. "It's *him.* I've been afraid to put him on hold."

"Him whom?" Swift asked, reaching for the phone.

"You know, *him*! The President."

"Well, Mary, lucky thing I came in just as he called."

"He's been on the phone about ten minutes," Mary said. "I told him you were out. He said he'd wait."

"Ten minutes?" Swift said, staring at the receiver in his hand with a snake-handler's respect. He brought it slowly up to his ear. "Hello?"

"Mr. Swift?" Not the President.

"That's right."

"One second." Which stretched to five minutes.

"Hello?" The President.

"Hello?"

"Nate? Where the hell you been, boy?"

"I've been out investigating, Mr. President. That's what you pay me for: to investigate."

"Damn right. And I got confidence in you, Nate. Confidence which had better not be misplaced. The country is counting on you, Nate. A fact which the country had better not ever find out. What have you got for me? You got IT yet?"

"No, Mr. President. But we have a lead. A start."

"I knew it. I knew I could rely on you. Let's hear it."

Swift told him about the coins. There was a silence, while the President digested the information. Then: "You're kidding!"

"How's that, Mr. President?"

"You're kidding. That's progress?"

"It's a connection. We had nothing before; now we have three gold coins."

There was a short pause, then the President abruptly hung up.

"Nice office," Ves said. "I've never been in your office before, you know that? Nice secretary." He smiled down at Mary, who was young, pretty and easily flattered by distinguished-looking older men who smiled without leering. She smiled back.

Nate put down the phone. "The President," he told Ves, "just hung up on me."

"You told him about the coins?" Ves asked.

"Yes."

"He is not amused?"

"Obviously he expected more. He's disappointed at the lack of progress."

"Your president," Ves said, with heavy accent on the

'your', "is a man who expects miracles. And clearly he has a right to: he got elected, didn't he?"

"He's afraid of what will happen if the people find out," Nate said.

"They already know," Ves told him. "It's hard to keep the results of presidential elections secret for long."

"Laugh," Swift said. "Go ahead. But he's right, you know. If the people find out the Constitution has mysteriously disappeared, there'll be panic in the streets. Look at it this way: aside from the symbolic importance of the document, if the Constitution, kept in a vault-tight building under constant guard, in a helium-filled bullet-proof case that's set to dive under concrete at the first sign of trouble, can silently vanish away, then what is safe, and where should it be kept?"

"Well, then, let us proceed to find the damn thing," Ves said. "If Tom Browne was willing to attempt 'What song the Sirens sang, or what name Achilles assumed when he hid himself among women', then surely we can try where the paper strayed, or what hand signed its replacement."

"I'm glad it will prove so easy," Swift said. "I had rather feared it would be difficult. What do we do?"

"Let me sit down and muse over a piece of paper for a few moments," Ves said, "and I'll tell you." He took off his jacket, a blue blazer with large gold buttons. He was about to hang it over the chair when he noticed the small coatrack in the corner and appropriated a hanger instead. "Like the jacket?" he asked Mary, who'd been watching the process. "I used to wear suits," he told her when she nodded, "but now that I'm retired—semi-retired —I wear what I like. My son wears the suits." He carried his vest-pocket notebook back to the chair and began doodling in it.

The office door opened, and a heavily bearded, skinny young man wearing a laboratory smock barged in. "Hello, Mary love, hello Mr. Swift. Here are your coins; we're all done with them." He slid the thin cigar box onto the desk.

"What's the word, Ralph?" Nate asked.

"Gold," Ralph replied solemnly, "solid gold. Well—an alloy, of course. They are each two hundred seventy grains troy weight, the U.S. standard for that denomination, with an accuracy of better than two parts in a thousand. They were stamped from a screw press, most probably; the compression patterns are different from those caused by a lever press. They show a very slight amount of wear, different for each coin, which is consistent with being in circulation for between six months and two years." Ralph paused here and looked up expectantly, waiting for some appropriate comment.

"Hum," Swift said, nodding his head, "hum. Go on."

"The coins are nine-one-six-point-six-four fine, which means they contain slightly over eight percent alloy. This fits in closely with the traditional eleven-twelfths gold standard for coinage, first adopted in England in 1526 and still in use. Except there haven't been any gold coins minted recently. The alloy is 95% copper, 4% tin, and 1% zinc. This is known as coinage bronze, which was adopted by most of the world's mints shortly after 1789, and used until nickel-bronze was introduced in 1861."

"Excuse me, young man," Ves said, "but are you saying that these coins were minted before 1861?"

"No, sir," Ralph said, sounding slightly shocked. "That would be most unscientific. I am merely saying that the alloy we found in the coins has not been in use since 1861. Also, the screw press has not been in use in government mints since the invention of the lever press in 1839 by Uhlhorn. Of course, some small private mint somewhere could still be using screw presses and alloying with coinage bronze."

"Do you know of any?" Swift asked.

"No, sir, And we keep comprehensive records."

"Thank you, Ralph. And thank the rest of the gang down in the lab for me. I appreciate your putting the rest of your work aside and getting this out for me."

"Our pleasure, sir," Ralph said. "Whenever we can do anything for you, sir, all of us below the stairs are only too anxious to please." He left the room, closing the door gently behind him.

"It's that damn union," Nate said, shaking his head. "Ever since those government scientists were unionized, you've practically had to kiss their collective Erlenmeyer flasks to get them to do anything."

"Here," Ves said, ripping a page out of his notebook, "the fruits of my intensive labors. Mary, if you can make out my handwriting, type this up. Then we'll Xerox it and send copies out right away."

"Copies of what?" Nate asked. "To where?"

"To all the papers," Ves explained. "Major papers all over the country. Just a simple advertisement for the book page. We always used to advertise for missing jewelry. It often worked. No explanations required; that sort of thing. The simpler the better."

Ves's ad read:

> Unusual information or documents wanted
> pertaining to Aaron Burr. Highest prices
> paid. Confidential. Box 1945, Washington D.C.
> 20013. (202) 301-3856

Nate shrugged, an uncharacteristic gesture. "I always thought you private detectives had all sorts of mysterious secrets. Now I found out you advertise. Another boyhood illusion shattered."

"Sherlock Holmes advertised," Mary said.

FOUR

They quickly received a wide variety of replies from all over the country. Most of these could be just as quickly eliminated:

SIRS: THEODOSIA BURR, AARONS ONLY DAUGHTER, NOT LOST AT SEA. AM TRY-ING TO ESTABLISH CLAIM TO THE VAST BURR ESTATE AS GREAT-GRANDSON OF ILLEGITIMATE SON OF THEODOSIA AND SLAVE ON ALEX. HAMILTON'S JAMAICA ESTATE WHERE SHE RAN TO HIDE FROM HER FATHER. WATER INTERESTS OUT TO STOP ME. LIQUIDS TRUST SPIES IN

EVERY GLASS AND JAR. NOT FOR ME, AGAINST ME. NEED TWO THOUSAND DOLLARS TO PURSUE CASE. REPLY IMMEDIATELY. CODE NAME BLUE.
JACKSON HAMILTON ADAMS BURR
CABLE ADDRESS JHAB

Gentlepersons,

I perused wih fascination your brief epistle in the *Abalone Morning Tribune* this past Thursday. How you found out about me I do not know, but it is obvious that you did; else why should you have an advertisement in such a backward, out of the way town as Abalone?

Yes, it is true, although I do not know how you discovered it. I am the woman for whom Aaron Burr refused the presidency and went off with to Mexico. They said it was treason, but it was love.

It all seems so long ago now. To look at me today, you would hardly believe that I could have provoked such passion in a man. But I was considered a beauty in my youth, and possessed of great charm and wit. Napoleon thought so, as did the Duke of Wellington, a very gracious man.

You will want to interview me. That I can, at long last, allow. But no pictures, and no persons from the press.

I await with sincerity your reply,

Bessie VanArwitt Lee

"—Do I have two-oh-two-three-oh-one-three-eight-five-six?

—That's right.

—I have a collect call for anyone from Mr. Dittle Parsons.

—Who?

—Mr. Dittle Parsons (tell him it's about Burr) Mr. Parsons says it is about—was that Burr? (that's right, Aaron Burr)—it is about Aaron Burr.

—Where's the call from?

—New York City.

—I'll accept the call.

—Go ahead please.

—Hello?

—You the people who want information about Aaron Burr?

—That's right. My name is Romero. What can I do for you?

—You got it wrong. It is I who can help you. I got the goods on this Burr.

—The goods?

—Right. You want info, and info I got. State your price.

—What sort of information do you have, Mr. Parsons?

—What's it worth for a look? Just let me tell you that I have all the Tammany records. *All* of them.

—I see, Mr. Parsons. Leave your number with my secretary, and we'll get back to you.

—Right. But you guys better make it fast. You're not the only ones interested, you know.

—Thank you for calling us first, Mr. Parsons."

But some of them proved of immediate interest:

Gentlemen,

I am a History teacher at DeWitt Clinton High School in New York City. The Bronx, to be precise. My son, Richard, is a stamp collector. He is only twelve years old, and has a limited allowance, so his collection is of necessity limited.

He recently obtained, at a high school fair, a fragment of brown wrapping paper containing three stamps. The stamps were hand-cancelled with a wavy-line pattern and a circle that reads GENERAL POST OFFICE NEW YORK CITY 4 JUNE 1923 PM. The three stamps are identical: light green printing on white paper. In the center of an oval is a head facing three-quarters forward with curly hair and a tight smile. Around the top of the oval are the words UNITED STATES POSTAGE. Around the bottom: Aaron Burr. Straight across the bottom: ONE DISME.

As you probably know, the United States Post Office has no record of ever issuing an Aaron Burr stamp.

Does this fit into the definition of "unusual information or document"? If so, what do you consider "Highest Prices" to be? My son would like to keep one of the

stamps, but would be willing to sell the other two to
help finance his collecting.

Sincerely yours,
Albert E. Gorey

Ves called up Mr. Gorey, negotiated a suitable price
with his son, Richard, for one of the stamps, and had
them mail it to him. It seemed to fit into the pattern,
although what the pattern might look like was still unknown. It wasn't like doing a jigsaw puzzle, but more like
trying to sort out the pieces to one puzzle from a box
containing a dozen.

That evening, Nate and Ves were sharing an after-
dinner brandy in Ves's study when Mrs. Montefugoni announced a caller. She described him as a 'gentleman', and
this was a term that she used rarely, so they awaited his
appearance in the study doorway with interest.

"Mr. Romero?" the caller asked, standing in the doorway and looking from one man to the other. He had a
finely-chiseled, patrician face with a strong nose and a
thin mouth which did not look pleased. His impeccably-
tailored clothing would have made him one of the best
dressed men at the inauguration of President Warren
Gamaliel Harding.

"I am Mr. Romero," Ves admitted. "Come in, sir.
What can I do for you?"

"I called this afternoon," the visitor said, "but you were
out. Your, ah, housekeeper suggested that I try this evening. It is, ah, in reference to your advertisement of three
days ago in the *New York Herald*. Or was it the *Times*?"

"The *New York Herald* has been out of existence for
about fifty-sixty years, I think," Swift said. "It became
part of the *Herald-Tribune*, then expired."

The visitor looked at him with a chilling glance. "Ah,
yes?" he said. "Then it clearly must have been the *Times*."

"You come in answer to the ad?" Ves said. "You have
information for me? Unusual documents concerning
Aaron Burr?"

"No, sir," the stranger said. "Allow me to clarify my
position. I have no current knowledge or documentation
concerning the whereabouts or intentions of that traitor,
Burr. I seek, rather, some information from you, and am
prepared to pay for it, and pay well."

Swift was about to make some angry reply to this, but Ves shut him up with a glance. "What sort of information can we give you?" Ves asked.

The man strode into the room and stopped in the center. He was not the sort of man you asked to sit down: he clearly sat or stood at his own pleasure. "Tell me who your client is," he said. "Tell me what his interest is, and tell me what you have discovered."

Ves nodded approvingly. "Concise," he said.

"It reminds me of a final I had in Psychology," Nate said. " 'Describe what you now know on this subject.' It certainly covers the ground."

The stranger glared at him. "Have you some objection to this particular ground being covered?" he demanded. "Do you side with the Cataline? The forces are gathering, the sides are being picked. Choose carefully, young man!" His voice resounded with the powerful tones of the expert public speaker, and his stature seemed to grow as his voice rang out.

"You should know I can't do that," Ves said mildly. "You're asking me to betray the identity of a client— if I have a client; to release confidential information, and reveal my sources. No self-respecting private detective would behave in such a fashion. Not if he expected to stay in business."

"I know nothing about the ethical considerations of your profession," the man said. "That is, if I may call it a profession. But your logic is specious. Your advertisement asked to purchase information of others, and this is fine and honorable. I ask the same of you, and you use words like 'betray' and 'reveal'. My gold is as good as the next man's."

"Gold?" Ves asked.

"If you wish," the man said. "Specie or paper. I have a strong interest in this matter, and will pay well for your help."

"I think we speak at cross purposes," Ves said. "I don't believe I have any information that would interest you."

"I will pay to be allowed to decide that for myself," the man insisted. He took a coin out of his pocket. "An eagle to know who employs you. A second to know what you have discovered."

Nate's gaze fastened on the gold coin. "I'd like to see that coin," he said.

The stranger closed his fist around it. "Earn it!"

Nate stared at Ves, who considered carefully for a minute. "I cannot tell you who we are working for," he told his guest. "That would be breaking confidence. But I will let you examine photocopies of the only two, ah, documents we have as yet uncovered."

"Fair enough, sir." The stranger flipped the coin over to Ves.

Ves picked two sheets of paper from the coffee table in front of him, turned them right side up, and handed them to his guest. One contained a front and back view of the Mexican coin, and the other a likeness of the *one disme* stamp.

The stranger stared at them. "This?" he asked. "These are your documents? You jest, sir, surely you jest."

"I told you that I didn't think I had anything that would interest you," Ves said. "That's it. We may, of course, receive any number of documents in response to our ad. If you'll tell me what in particular you are interested in discovering, perhaps I could call you if we find out anything." He pocketed the coin.

"I assumed you knew, sir," the stranger said. "The tenor of your advertisement . . . is it possible that you are unaware? Does the term 'prime time' mean anything to you?"

"You mean TV?" Swift asked.

"TV?" the stranger repeated, as though it were a completely foreign term.

"Yes, the networks—"

"Exactly!" The stranger pounced on the term. "The network—prime time; you do know. I thought you must. Well, sir, I am the Great Antagonist."

He stood there in the center of the room, a little puffed up, waiting for the proper response. The look he saw on the faces of the two men must have satisfied him. "I see you are surprised, eh? Never thought to meet me, eh? Well, I'm human, gentlemen; I'll tell you that. I'm human. And your little advertisement intrigued me. Pure luck that I'd happen to see it, of course. But I just happened to be here. Won't be for long, though; have to travel elsewhen soon." He paused and thought for a second.

"If you do find anything," he continued, "I'll leave a number that will eventually reach me. Remember: my pay is liberal. And if you can ever find it in your ethical heart to reveal who employs you and why, I should be most fascinated. Most.

"I must take my leave. You can reach me here." He scribbled a number onto a pasteboard card and twirled it onto the table in front of Ves. "I thank you for your time, gentlemen." He bowed slightly and exited abruptly. A second later they heard the front door open and close.

Swift went suspiciously into the hall to make sure that their guest had, indeed, departed. When he returned, Ves had fished the gold eagle from his pocket and was examining it under the light.

"Well?" Nate demanded. "Whose picture is on this one?"

"A lady with a turban," Ves said. "Name of 'Liberty', it says here. Get me my handbook of U.S. Coins, will you? In the reference shelf over there—toward the bottom."

Nate retrieved the indicated book and Ves flipped through it. "Here we are," he said. "Hm. Hmm."

"What?"

"It's a real coin, so says the book," Ves said.

"That's a relief," Nate said.

"Dated 1797," Ves said. "Very common thing to carry around."

"Eccentric," Swift said.

"According to the handbook," Ves said, "this little circle of gold goes for over two grand these days."

"What?"

"Two thousand dollars," Ves said. "I'll buy dinner. Except that we're already eaten dinner. Tomorrow I'll buy dinner."

"Crazy," Swift said. He bent over and picked up the pasteboard the stranger had left.

"I have the faint glimmerings of an idea," Ves said, "but it's too nebulous and too insane to discuss just yet."

"Perhaps this will help," Swift said, holding the pasteboard card up before Ves's eyes.

A phone number was neatly printed in ink on the back. On the front:

ALEX: HAMILTON
Attorney

FIVE

||||||||||||||||||||||||||||

The winds were sudden and off the sea: cold, snippy winds that blew up your pants leg and tugged at your greatcoat. They seemed to be omnidirectional. Wherever you stood they found you; whatever you hid behind, they whipped around in playful little cold spurts. It was time for taking in the brass monkeys, for covering the pool tables. And it wasn't quite winter yet. Winters in Washington tend to be mild, but the last spurts of autumn can be pretty fierce.

Swift stood concealed in a doorway, stamping his feet, keeping his hands crossed under his arms, and wishing he'd worn two extra sweaters. Across the street, in the brownstone he was watching, nothing was stirring. It was almost ten a.m., and the house was as mute and dark as it had been at five. Or, for that matter, at four. Both hours Nate remembered very well.

It had been three o'clock in the morning before Ves, Nate, and the President had been able to get the address that matched with the phone number written on the back of Alex: Hamilton's card. It would have been faster if they had asked the FBI to get the address from the phone company, but the President wouldn't ask the FBI for anything. They would only have insisted on knowing what it was for. Ever since Watergate, they'd been funny that way, the bastards.

So Ves Romero, Nate Swift, and the President of the United States went painstakingly through the Metropolitan Washington, District of Columbia Section phone book until, with a cry of "eureka", and a sweeping gesture that knocked a cut-glass bowl full of macadamia nuts off the table, Ves announced that he had found the number. It was listed as a Mrs. Buffie O'Gorman at an address on V Street, Northwest.

While searching their thirds of the phone book, they

had discussed what Alex: Hamilton's visit had meant, and
who he really was. It was a conundrum more complex
than the ancient riddle of who shaved the barber, but the
answer was the same: follow him around and see. And so,
at four in the morning Nate took up his station across
the street from the house hopefully holding both Mrs.
Buffie O'Gorman and Mr. Alex: Hamilton.

It had been cold at four, but Nate knew that as the
sun's rays came up, the air would warm up. Nate was
wrong. It got colder during the morning, and Nate felt
as if the hairs on the back of his hand would shatter
and fall off if he closed his fist. The brightly-shining morning sun was a sham, a million fireflies in an ice-cold jar,
rising slowly above the frigid towers of Washington office
buildings in the distance.

And the V Street brownstone, haughtily drawn up to
its full three stories, glared down at him through icy upper
windows, daring him to aproach its front steps. Or, perhaps he was just a bit light-headed from too many hours
spent standing in the cold.

A car cruised past him, and Nate recognized Ves's
profile as the car turned the corner. A minute later, Ves
rounded the corner and walked up the steps to the doorway Nate was loitering in. He paused and studiously
examined the names on the mailboxes. "Anything?" he
whispered.

"Where the hell have you been?" Swift demanded, carefully looking disinterestedly away.

"Getting things set up," Ves said. "Any motion?"

"Neither fish nor fowl," Swift said. "I'm freezing. And
I'm starting to hallucinate. I think I just had an argument
with the building across the street. It doesn't like me
loitering here. Come to think of it, I don't, either. I go
home and go to sleep now, right, Big Brother?"

"Not yet," Ves told him, "but soon, soon. We have to
get someone to relieve you."

"What about the Secretary of State?" Nate growled.

"You think that's funny?" Ves demanded. "The President wanted to come out here himself."

"I won't stop him," Nate said. "Although he could
never keep awake in school. We'd double date, and he'd
fall asleep coming home."

"The girls must have loved him," Ves said.

"We all did," Nate said. "Most of the time, he was

doing the driving. Still, if the President is anxious enough to want to relieve me here, I think it would be in the National Interest."

"I wouldn't let him come," Ves said regretfully. "But I would love to have seen it: the bulletproof limousine around the corner with the Marine sergeant chauffeur huddled up in the front seat trying to keep warm. The President sitting on a camp stool in this doorway, with a camp table in front of him, warming his hands over a cup of cocoa. Two Secret Service men loitering inconspicuously in front of the house; two more dangling from the roof. The President's mobile information post set up in the ground floor front apartment, much to the bewilderment . . . no, strike that—the tenant would have been evacuated by the Secret Service. And the crowd of newsmen back on the other side of the police line which they'd have to set up. Or, perhaps they'd just blockade the street at both ends. Luckily, none of this is anything that Alex would notice."

"I love it when you get sarcastic," Nate said. "You sound just like W.C. Fields."

"Yes, yes," Ves said. "Here, take this." He handed Swift what looked like a brown map-pin without turning around.

"What is it?" Nate asked.

"Communications device," Ves said. "The President dug up a few of them. Stick it behind your lapel, or somewhere within half a meter of your mouth. Now, take this small spot bandage and press it firmly to the skin behind your ear."

"Which one?" Swift asked.

"I don't suppose it matters," Ves said. "Now all you have to do is touch the button to send a message to me. The receiver is on all the time, of course."

"What's the range on these things?" Swift asked, trying to look natural as he massaged the spot behind his left ear.

"A little over a kilometer if conditions are just right; a lot less if they're not."

"FBI?" Swift asked.

"Don't be silly."

"CIA?"

"Department of Fish and Game," Ves told him. "Use them to track partridge or talk to trout, or some such."

"We don't have anything like this over at the Bureau

of Weights and Measures Observational Branch," Nate said sadly. "But then, the B.W.M.O.B. doesn't speak to many trout.'"

Just then, there was a flash of movement behind the glass front door of the brownstone. Alex: Hamilton, immaculate in homburg, cutaway gray jacket, vest, pleated gray pants with six-inch cuffs, and gray spats over patent-leather black shoes, strode out. "Quick," Ves said. "You follow him. I'll interrogate the landlady while he's out."

"I don't know if I'm up to it," Swift said. "I haven't had much sleep."

"I'll get a relief man to you as quickly as possible," Ves assured him. "Just don't lose him."

Nate plodded inconspicuously after Alex:, and Ves went down the street to a luncheonette to call the President. Then he called his son at Romero Associates to arrange relief for Nate—his son promised him an operative by two in the afternoon—then Ves sat down and ate a small breakfast: poached egg, toast, and a glass of low fat milk. Then he went back up the block and rang the bell of the brownstone.

A short, dumpy woman with startlingly orange hair, wearing a passion-pink housecoat, appeared out of one of the side rooms and came to the door. Clutching a broom firmly in her left hand, she peered through the glass panel at Ves. "Yes?" she mouthed through the door.

"Mrs. O'Gorman?" Ves asked politely. "I wonder if I might ask you a few questions?"

"What?" she mouthed. He couldn't hear her, and it was clear that she couldn't hear him.

"A few questions!" Ves stated loudly at the door.

The lady mouthed something more, in obvious agitation, and waved the broom up and down a few times for emphasis. Ves couldn't hear a sound from inside the door.

"Open the door," Ves said, carefully moving his lips to the pattern of the words, "open the door."

"Arb grab aaab!" the lady mouthed firmly from behind the closed door. Finally however, seeing that none of this was driving Ves away, she did open the door to the extent permitted by her chain lock. "No more rooms!" she announced firmly, squeezing as much of her face as she could into the crack.

"Information, not a room, I want," Ves said hurriedly

and ungrammatically, before she could slam the door. "I'll pay!"

"Pay?" The word caught her attention. "How much? What do you want to know? Let's see the money."

Ves took a ten-dollar bill out of his pocket and waved it in front of her. Her little eyes lit up, and she took the chain off the door. "Come in," she said.

"I'd like some information on your tenant," Ves said. "The gentleman who left about an hour ago."

"Come, sit down," the lady said. "Have a cup of coffee. What do you want to know?"

Ves came into the kitchen with her and accepted a rose floral cup of a watery brown liquid he couldn't identify. "Anything you know about him," Ves said. "How long he's been here, what he does during the day, any visitors he has had; is there anything at all unusual about him."

"A week tomorrow," the woman told him. "I don't know what he does, but he brings home books and magazines and papers all the time. No visitors and nothing unusual. Is that worth ten bucks?"

Ves handed her the bill. "Nothing else?" he asked. "Nothing out of the ordinary?"

"Very quiet man," the landlady said. "Gave me rent a week in advance. In gold."

"Gold?" Ves said, his voice betraying his fascination with this bit of news.

"It's legal," she said. "I checked."

"A coin?" Ves asked.

"What then, a nugget?"

"Mexican?" Ves asked.

"I wouldn't take no foreign money," the landlady declared with patriotic virtue, fishing out the coin and displaying it in the stubby fingers. It, indeed, was not foreign. An eagle, minted in Philadelphia in 1833, it was as American as the president whose face was on the front: Alexander Hamilton.

"Hamilton never was President of the United States," Ves said, half to himself.

"That's what *you* say. That's my coin and you give it back right now!" she exclaimed. And forthwith she reclaimed it.

"*Ves! Can you get over here right away?*" the patch behind Ves's ear asked in Nate's voice.

"Where?" Ves asked, touching the button.

"What?" asked the landlady.

"There's a Turkish bath on North Dakota and Y," Nate's voice said.

"Y?" Ves asked.

"Why not?" the landlady demanded. "Gold always has to go up in value because there isn't enough of it to make earrings, now that pierced ears are coming back. You can't use tin because it will rot your earlobe off."

"That's right, Y," Swift said. *"I'll meet you in front."*

"Okay," Ves said.

"I should think so," the landlady said. "My step-daughter-in-law told me that. And she should know: she's in training to become a beautician."

"Thank you, Mrs. O'Gorman, you've been a big help," Ves said, preparing to take his hurried leave.

"Also silver, but not as much," she said, taking the cup from his hand. "Come again."

SIX

||||||||||||||||||||||||||||

Swift followed Alex: as easily as a trailer follows a truck. The man strode down the street as disdainful of cars or pedestrians as though he had written assurance of a place in the hereafter. He never glanced to the right or left, and if the world behind him had been dismantled and crated as soon as he passed he would not have known it. Nate could have dressed in a clown suit and rode on the neck of an elephant three paces behind, and Alex: would still have marched on obliviously. Which was a good thing: in Nate's present state of exhaustion, the subtler methods of tailing would have been beyond him. But he was able to stagger on, maintaining a more-or-less steady ten meters behind his subject.

Alex: went into a branch library. Nate checked for other possible exits and, finding none, settled down happily on a bus stop bench to await Alex:'s return. The only problem was that as soon as Nate sat down, he felt himself drifting into the euphoric pre-sleep state where the eyes close of their own volition and fantasy and reality erase their common border. Nate stood up to stamp his feet and stop from going to sleep, but just then Alex: Hamilton came out of the library.

He had changed clothes while inside, and was now wearing a brown frock coat with wide lapels and matching vest, a white silk cravat, brown knee breeches with white stockings, and leather slip-ons with great brass buckles. He carried a cocked hat under his arm and wore a white periwig on his head. He walked by muttering, "I'm late, I'm late, the General will have my head." Nate tried to follow him, but found that he couldn't move, seeming to be frozen in one spot. He tried to move, he willed himself to move, he strained to move, then his head fell forward onto his knee and he woke up.

This time he did jump to his feet and stamp around. He pinched himself in the lobe of the ear to make sure that he was really awake, and hoped that Alex: had not left the library in the minute or so that he had dozed.

Luck was with him, and two minutes later Alex: emerged, trotted down the front steps, and strode down the street. Swift took up the pursuit.

A few ground-eating minutes later Alex: arrived at the VENUS-ADONIS Turkish Bath and entered. "Who would have believed?" Nate thought, as he settled down outside to wait. The problem was finding a comfortable position that wouldn't put him to sleep. After a few minutes of fidgeting, he decided that any position would put him to sleep; the only hope was to keep in motion. He walked back and forth in front of the VENUS-ADONIS's front door, trying not to look like a shy fan or a process server. He shifted to the bank across the street, walking back and forth in front of its massive doors until he noticed a man with a formal mustache, thin, humorless lips, and a nervous, jumpy gaze peering at him suspiciously through the open blinds in the bank's front window. Then he moved back to the VENUS-ADONIS.

All of a sudden, a clock of realization parted the surrounding fog of tiredness and woke him up completely. Swift remembered that he hadn't performed the first and most basic check; the kindergarten lesson of the plainclothesmen and spies. He had not looked for other exits.

He stuck an empty pop bottle before the front door, walked around the corner quickly, and located the alley that ran to the back of VENUS-ADONIS. There was a loading platform that clearly hadn't been used in many years, with a large roll-up door which was padlocked on the outside. The small door to the side of the platform opened from the inside, but there were two garbage cans in front of it. From the position of the detritus surrounding the cans it was clear that no one had moved them recently.

Thus reassured, Nate ran back around the corner to catch Alex: if he should have started to leave while Nate was inspecting the garbage. There was no sign of him, and the pop bottle was still in place; meaning he was either still inside, or subtle beyond all expectation.

By now Swift was beginning to worry. Unless Alex: was indulging in some of the more exotic pleasures, or had fallen asleep in the steam bath, he should have reappeared by now; it had been over an hour. Some people spent the better part of a day in that sort of establishment, but Alex: was too busy and too purposeful to be sidetracked for long by material indulgence.

Nate pushed through the swinging doors and entered the white-tiled lobby. He approached the white-coated attendant behind the white-tiled counter in one corner. "Morning," he said.

"Sci-fi buffs," the man muttered, scratching his nose with the tip of his pencil.

"How's that?" Swift asked.

The man looked up. "Oh, I didn't see you. I was just looking for a three-letter word meaning 'sci-fi buffs'."

"Good luck," Nate said. "The man who came in here about an hour ago; do you know where he went? Very neatly dressed . . . "

"The cat with the homburg?" The attendant pointed his pencil. "Down the corridor and to the left. Steam room. You a friend of his?"

"I know him," Nate said cautiously, "why?"

"He went into the steam room, you know?"

"You told me," Nate said.

"Yeah. Well, he went into the steam room. I told him he'd have to wait a minute while I got the steam turned on, 'cause he was the first customer of the day. He said he didn't want the steam turned on. I asked him if he wanted to use the locker room and hang his clothes up, and he said no to that too; which, I suppose figures if he didn't want the steam turned on. You know? He's been in there ever since, fully dressed, with no steam."

"He didn't come out?" Swift asked.

"He didn't come past me," the attendant told him, "and there's no rear door to the steam room. He could have got into the locker room, but that opens out onto this corridor also, you know?"

"I wonder what he's doing in there," Swift mused. The attendant shrugged. If it wasn't a seven-letter word meaning "dealing with in an aggressive, unjust, or spiteful manner", he wasn't interested. He went back to his puzzle.

"He's been an awfully long time," Swift said.

"Feel free to go back and make sure he's all right," the attendant said.

"I wouldn't want him to think I was being nosy," Nate said.

"Peek in," the attendant suggested. "There's a glass panel in the door. When the steam's on you can't see anything, but since your buddy didn't want the steam on . . . "

Nate walked back to the steam room door and peered through the glass. At first he couldn't see anything in the all-white room; it was like being snow blind. Then details emerged: the whitewashed wooden bench, the pattern of tiles on the wall, the drains, the pipes, the door to the locker room, and the fact that there wasn't a soul inside.

He pushed the door open and went in. There was no place to hide in the large, square room but under the benches, and no one was doing that. He walked through into the locker room. There were four rows of lockers, all of them unlocked and most of them open. There were two wide shelves stacked with bath towels. There was no Alex: but Swift opened the closed lockers, feeling that he should go through the motions. He knew Alex: Hamilton wasn't hiding in one of them. He was right.

Swift didn't panic. He was too experienced, too intelligent, too rational, too blasé, too tired to panic. He walked with measured tread back to the counter. "He's gone," he announced.

The attendant looked up from his puzzle. "Huh?"

"He's gone. The gentleman with the homburg."

"That's silly," the attendant said, looking annoyed. "He hasn't come out. He must be in the locker room."

"I looked. He's not."

"The massage rooms? They're across the corridor. But they're supposed to be locked. The masseuses aren't in yet." He took a key ring from a drawer in the counter and deserted his puzzle to try the three doors. They were all locked. He opened them. There was no one inside. "Funny," he said. He went back to his puzzle.

"Ves," Nate called into the button in his lapel, "Can you get over here right away?"

SEVEN

Ves examined the building, then he examined the attendant, then he examined Nate. "One of the three of you," he concluded, "is mistaken—or lying."

"The building?" Swift asked. "Isn't that an extreme form of personification, to say that a building is either mistaken or lying?"

"Only in so far as it expresses the wishes of its builder or owner," Ves explained, settling down on one of the metal benches in the lobby and glaring at the white walls. "For instance, it could be mistakenly leading us to the conclusion that there is no other exit to the steam room; innocently concealing another behind a crate, or masking it as an air duct. Or, it could be lying to us and have a concealed door."

"A secret panel?" Swift asked. "I thought that was only a fictional device. Are there any real secret panels?"

"Of course," Ves said. "There are hidden doors of all descriptions and for all purposes. There are the priest-holes in England, which were used, I believe, during the time of Cromwell. There are hidden rooms in pioneer houses, so the family could disappear in case of an overwhelming Indian attack. There are the rooms used during the time of the Underground Railroad. There are hidden doors in some executive suites today, which conceal a bathroom, a bedroom, or merely a bar."

"No secret panels in here," the attendant said, displaying an interest in what was happening for the first time. "I checked for that."

Ves turned to him. "You did what?" he asked. "Why should you do anything like that?"

" 'Cause of the other two," the attendant explained. "I mean, it seemed like the reasonable explanation at the time."

Nate stared at him. "The other two?" He was almost afraid to find out what the attendant meant.

"Right," the attendant said. "Two other gentlemen have come through here and never come out. That's just while I'm on duty. First one came after I'd been here about a month; that would be about two years ago. This guy dressed like an Italian comes barging in here and rushes through into the steam room. I run after him to give him a ticket and time-stamp him in, and when I come into the room he's gone. And I'm no more than maybe two-three seconds behind."

"Gone?" Nate asked.

"What do you mean, 'like an Italian?' " Ves demanded.

"Was the room empty?" Nate asked.

"Like a—you know—Roman. Like he'd just come off a movie set. With the funny-looking armor and the kilt and the leggings: like that. There was another guy in the room, laying down with a towel over his face. He says he heard the door open and felt the draft, but didn't see anyone, because he had a towel on his face."

"A Roman?" Ves repeated.

"I called the police," the attendant said. "But that was sure a mistake. Two guys came out to question me. One of them decided I must have made the whole thing up and there was no guy; the other one thinks maybe I killed the guy and got rid of the body. They made me look through a couple thousand pictures and tell me they'll keep in touch. That's the last I hear. So the next time, I don't call no one."

"The next time . . . " Swift said.

"Yeah. 'I shall make use of your facility,' he says, flipping me this gold coin and trotting into the steam room. I thought he meant something dirty, talking like that. I was about to go after him and tell him we didn't do that kind of thing, but I was distracted by the coin. It was a stella, and I'd never seen one. Run across the word in puzzles all the time."

"Stella?" Swift asked.

"A four-dollar gold piece. There were less than five hundred of them minted. That's what the guy I sold it to said. There's a large star on the back and the word *stella,* that's Latin for star."

"Whose picture is on the front?" Ves asked.

"Liberty. With her hair down. Kind of a chubby-looking face."

"What happened to the gentleman who gave you the coin?" Ves asked.

"Have no idea. He never came out of the steam room. That's when I started searching for hidden panels, but I did a careful cross-check of the room sizes, and there'd be nowhere for a panel to go."

"So no panels," Nate said.

The attendant shrugged. "Maybe a panel," he said, "but it don't go anywhere."

"So where did those three men disappear to?" Nate demanded, getting slightly annoyed with the attendant's matter-of-fact attitude.

The attendant put his lips together and pushed them in and out for a minute. "I thought a lot about that," he said. "Did you ever hear of the fourth dimension?"

Ves shook his head. "This approaches the sublime," he said. "It has certainly passed the ridiculous. If I assume the good faith of both of you, if not the good sense, I must conclude that the secret of the disappearance—of the three disappearances—is a secret of the building." He waggled a finger at the attendant. "Do you know how old it is?" he asked. "When it was built—and by whom?"

"Long time ago," the attendant said. "Guy named Pronzini worked here when I started. Retired last year, after forty years. Can you feature that—forty years. Started a chicken farm. He told me before the war this used to be a fancy place. I guess that would be World War Two."

"This place dates back to the twenties at least," Ves said. "Maybe a couple of decades older than that. They haven't built these palaces of pleasure for some time."

"Yeah," the attendant said. "That's what I thought."

"Well, we'll just look around," Ves said. "You can

never tell what they thought it was essential to build into a place like this, back in those far off days."

"I looked," the attendant said.

"I'm sure you did," Swift told him.

"But it's our job," Ves said. "You wouldn't want to stop us from doing our job, would you? You understand."

"Oh," the attendant said. "Of course." He went back behind the counter and picked up his puzzle. "Go ahead, do what you like. I hope you find something. It would sure be nice to be able to prove I'm not crazy." Pencil poised, he looked up at them. "I'm not, you know."

"I know," Nate said. "I saw him this time, remember."

"That's right," the attendant said happily, settling down to his puzzle. "Search away, gentlemen."

Ves led Nate into the steam room. "Tap the wall," he said.

"What for?" Nate asked.

"Didn't they teach you anything in Coast Guard Intelligence School besides *port* and *starboard*?"

"There is no Coast Guard Intelligence School," Nate told him. "There was one once, but it got misplaced. I was sent to Army Intelligence School at Fort Geronimo, Kansas."

"Having been associated with this government for some time in my youth," Ves said, "I am, somehow, not surprised."

"Went there for a year," Nate told him. "Picked up a lot of useful skills. Tank recognition—they were big on tank recognition. Order of battle, uniforms of foreign officers, chain of command, marching, crawling over barbed wire, saluting, and playing poker; those were the major skills they stressed."

"What about raping and looting?" Ves asked.

"It wasn't in my curriculum," Nate said. "Only career Army officers took it. It was a seminar, I believe. Why am I tapping the walls?"

"Listen," Ves told him. "If there's a hollow space, or anything else funny behind the wall, it will sound different. Here, watch!" He went around the wall with his ear pressed against it, tapping it every few inches. It gave a solid *thunk*.

The solid *thunk* continued everywhere either of them tapped, all around the wall, high and low. Ves finally stopped and glared accusingly at the ceiling. "Let's try the locker room," he said.

Nate worked his way around the locker room walls, while Ves tried inside the lockers, over the lockers, and under them. "Incredible!" Ves said finally, sitting down on the wooden bench. "He came in here, he came not out of here, but he is here not. And my grammar isn't nearly as mixed up as my mind right now. There must be a way. And if there is, I can find it; I know I can!"

"I believe you," Swift said. "Where do we look now?"

"Let's just stand back and examine these rooms," Ves said. "Not search them, but look at them: see what they look like. See if they differ in any way from what they should look like. See if there is anything unusual or different about the rooms, no matter how subtle. Sherlock Holmes once solved a difficult case by noting how deep the parsley had sunk into the butter."

"Right," Nate said, "different it is."

"Don't humor me," Ves said. "If you have a better idea, let's have it."

"That's the difference between you and Sherlock Holmes," Nate said. "He wouldn't ever have acknowledged that there might be a better idea." They both went back into the steam room and stood in the middle, staring at the four bare walls.

"Bare walls," Nate said.

"Except for the steam pipes and valve," Ves amended, "and that design carved into the tile."

"Strange little device," Nate said, going over to the waist-high pattern and examining it. "It looks like the decorative friezework they did in the New York subway stations during the depression. A little WPA in the steam room, do you think?"

The design was a simple one: a circle pieced out in green tile with a T inscribed in it in gold. "Probably the initial of the original owner," Ves said.

"You said anything different," Nate said.

"I know, I know," Ves came over and peered at the device, "but I didn't mean . . . say, you know the grout between the tiles looks different here—and here. Well, how do you like that?"

"What?" Swift demanded.

"Look here; all around here, where the green circle

meets the outside tiles. The grout is a different shade of white from anywhere else. It's darker, grayer."

"You're right!" Swift said. "Now why would that be?" He pulled a penknife out of his pocket and began attempting to pry around the outside of the green circle. "Too tight," he said. "Won't go in—wait a minute—push here—ahh!—just a little—nope—but—ahh!—There, it . . . shit!"

"What happened?" Ves asked. "Get it in?"

"Broke the blade," Swift told him. "Still, it shows that something does fit in there."

"Well, then there should be a way to open it," Ves said. He pushed and prodded, twisted and turned, tried different combinations of the above, and was suddenly rewarded: the wall opened at the green circle, revealing a hole the size and shape of a wall safe.

"What did you do?" Nate asked.

"I'm not sure," Ves told him, "but it worked."

Inside the opening was a Bakelite panel with three vernier dials with large handles set in a triangle, a glass-covered pointer dial in the middle, and a red light bulb, unlit, above the pointer. Below the triangle was a brass plate:

FRANKLYN & WHITNEY MODEL IV I. T.
all warranties, express & implied, are void if machine is tampered with. Contact our recent representative.

41-5734 e
FOR PRIME TIME DO NOT REDIAL

And below the brass plate was one black button.

"What the hell?" Nate wondered aloud.

"The steam?" Ves asked, then answered: "No. The steam valves are over there, and this looks vaguely electrical."

"Prime time," Nate said. "That's what Alex: was talking about, remember?"

"What do you suppose happens when you push that button?" Ves asked.

"I have no idea," Nate said. "You think it's the way Alex: got out of here?"

"Can you think of anything else?"

"No. Shall we push it?"

"Well," Ves considered. "Would you rather face the unknown, or the President?"

"I'll push it. Should we mess with the controls?"

"Just push the button."

Nate reached forward and pushed. It went firmly all the way in, then clicked.

The red light went on.

EIGHT

|||||||||||||||||||||||||||||

"Nothing seems to have happened," Swift said, after a minute of staring at the red light.

"We don't know that," Ves said. "We don't know what was supposed to happen. Maybe it has."

Nate shook his head. "We'd better get back to the office," he said. "Perhaps someone has found something: a coin with the head of Amelia Bloomer, or a stamp with a picture of President Dewey."

"I guess you're right," Ves said, "but we'll have to send a technical crew out here to examine this thing." He swung the tile door closed.

There was a slight shudder, as of a distant earthquake, or a passing subway train.

NINE

|||||||||||||||||||||||||||||

The corridor was not the same. The corridor had changed. It was an altogether different corridor: longer, for one thing, and wider, with more doors leading off it. In place of the white tile motif, there was red-flocked wallfabric, and gleaming brass gas fixtures; a high-pile maroon carpet down the center, and a cream-white ceiling.

"Nate . . ." Ves said, stopping in the steam room doorway and flinging out his arms to block the door.

"I see it," Swift said. "Something did happen."

"Don't go out there," Ves said. "Let's go back and push that button again; maybe it will go away."

"Can't," Swift said. "Remember what you said: the unknown or the President. Besides, how do we know that pushing the button again will take us back—maybe it will just take us further away."

"You're right," Ves said, releasing his grip on the sides of the door. "I guess I'm getting old and set in my ways. This should be no more frightening than a—an elevator. Just a new way of getting from one place to another. Just like being in an elevator, only the room's bigger."

"Not the room," Nate said, "just us."

"What?"

"It didn't move the room, it just moved us. Look around."

Ves looked back into the steam room. "You're right," he said. "The room is longer, and it has another row of benches. I didn't notice. But that circle-T is still there. Let's go find out what's happening, what that machine is, and where we are."

"You think the Constitution is here?"

"I refuse to speculate," Ves said. "But we're sure on the way to finding out what happened to it. And I'll bet you old Alex is about here somewhere."

They went down the newly-decorated corridor, across an elaborate entrance hall filled with couches, stuffed chairs, and massive chandeliers, and out into the street. The street was like a trough lined with tall buildings, running straight off in both directions until it disappeared at the convergence point to the left, and terminated in a park five blocks away on the right. It was pillared with tall telephone poles, and roofed with layers of wire crisscrossing in every direction.

The many vehicles in the street: cabs, buses, coaches, wagons, and a multitude of others, were mostly horse-drawn; although an occasional monstrous, horse-free contrivance did chug, snort, whistle, thump, clack, or screech by.

The sidewalk was crowded with pedestrians, who

streamed by in both directions, without pausing or keeping to either side. The few rules of passage seemed to be sex-based, as follows:

Women: maintain speed, keep eyes firmly fixed forward, use umbrellas as prods, do not stop, do not apologize, do not notice.

Men: tip hat, pass on left, do not stare.

The standard dress of these busy pedestrians was a sort of music hall Victorian. The men wore suits that buttoned up to the neck, with high starched shirt collars that cut in under the chin, and wide solid-colored cravats. They all wore hats: fedoras, toppers, crushers, planters, derbys, polo caps, miners' caps, visor caps, yacht caps, hunter caps, Eton caps, Russian admiral caps, and a few variants which have never been properly named.

The ladies, over their corsets, wore wide-shouldered, puffy-sleeved blouses, toe-length skirts, and pointy, high-heeled shoes. Each lady draped a cloak or cape over her blouse. Each carried an umbrella, as each man carried a cane.

Swift grabbed Ves by the arm. "Where are we?" he whispered. "Where the hell *are* we?"

"When," Ves corrected. "*When.*"

"What?"

The street darkened, as a large object occluded the sun. Ves looked up and saw the orange rays of the afternoon sun form a corona around a silver, cigar-shaped balloon which was pushing its nose into the latticework of a tall, open, iron tower atop a nearby building. Several men were busy, both on the tower and on the balloon-ship, connecting mooring lines.

"I take it back," Ves said. "*When* isn't right, either. What's left?"

"What is this place?" Swift demanded.

"Yes, that's one way of phrasing it," Ves agreed. "Now, how do we find out? I think, for one thing, we shouldn't remain as conspicuously dressed as we are. When we blend in better, we can go around asking discreet questions. That is, if the local populace speaks English. Or Italian—I think I can still get along in Italian."

Swift took a deep breath. "I can settle that," he said. He stepped into the stream of traffic and intercepted a man. "Excuse me, sir," he said, walking alongside his target, "could you please tell me what time it is?"

The man stared at him as if he were newly escaped from the place to which they send you when you start giggling a lot and carrying an axe in to dinner.

"Italiano?" Swift demanded desperately. *"La France? Sprechen Zie Deutsche? Panyamayish po-Russkie?"* The man shuddered slightly and continued on, ignoring Swift completely.

"Excuse me, sir . . ." Swift tried another gentleman.

". . . the time?" and another.

"Bitte, Meinherr . . ."

". . . a-t-il?"

A woman sniffed and clutched her umbrella even more firmly. "The idea!" she was heard to mutter as she passed by.

"English," Ves said.

"I was beginning to wonder," Swift said, retreating to the safety of the doorway.

"You know I'm not a negative person," Ves said, speaking slowly and distinctly, "but I wonder if it might not be wise to return to the steam room and see whether that button would return us to our own time—place—ah, home. We could come back better prepared for this investigation."

"I think we should continue," Swift said. "The longer we wait, the colder grows Alex's trail. And consider the President. A man who is not firm of mind and resolute of purpose to the point of insanity does not get to be President of the United States."

"I suppose you're right," Ves admitted. "As one gets older, one grows less fond of sudden, severe, disorienting shocks. But we live in an age when the unusual has become commonplace, and the unique has become expected. But I never expected anything like this. Oh well, I suppose the steam room can always be retreated to at need. Note the location firmly in your head, Nate. We'll use this as our rendezvous in case we get separated."

"What about our little radios?" Swift wondered. He touched the button on his lapel and recited: "One—two—three—do you hear me?"

"I hear you, I hear you," Ves said. "But remember, the range of these things isn't that great. However, they may prove useful. Now first things first: costumes. We must acquire adequate dress if we are to remain here."

"How do you suggest we do that?" Swift asked.

"Purchase," Ves said. "If there are any clothing stores that are still open. Incidentally, did you notice that we seem to have dropped about five hours? I think it was around noon when I met you at the VENUS-APOLLO."

Swift looked at his watch. "Two fifteen," he said. "And it's definitely late afternoon here. Ves, what the hell has happened to us?"

"Ours is not to reason why," Ves said. "Remember, somewhere at the other end of that gadget in the steam room is the President of the United States. And he is not pleased."

Swift nodded. "Let us go then, you and I," he said, and the two of them headed down the street.

The clothing store they found a block and a half away had ready-made everything, although the concept of size seemed to be a bit rudimentary. However, the salesman was a tailor, quite ready and willing to do any alterations necessary on his patented sewing contraption in the back room. Ves picked out a deep red suit, with an attractive waistcoat (*not* a vest, the tailor assured him, although people would use the word) with gold buttons. Swift found a green suit with lapels wide enough to cut a second jacket.

"Visitors from some foreign country, are you?" the tailor asked.

"Quite right," Ves admitted.

"And where would that be?" the tailor asked.

"Hard to say," Swift said.

"What's that?" the tailor asked, suspiciously.

"Difficult to pronounce," Swift amended. "Kwarshimi-bundi, we call it. Means 'Great Friendly Land By Water-fall with Many Snakes.' Of course, we all speak English now."

"Umph," the tailor said, chalking white lines all over the back of Ves's jacket. "Been in New York long?"

"New York?" Swift asked, unable to keep the surprise from showing in his voice.

"That's what we call it," the tailor said. "It means high taxes, high rents, a lot of damn micks and other foreigners —present company excepted, of course—moving in and taking the bread out of honest men's faces. Tammany at the back of it, without a doubt." He took a vicious swipe across the seat of Swift's trousers with the chalk. "Now, if you gentlemen will get out of those garments, I'll have the alterations done in half an hour." He went off to his sewing machine, a giant, clanking brute, that took up one whole corner of the back room.

It occurred to Swift somewhen during the purchasing and fitting of the suits, that whatever this place was, it was unlikely that the money he had in his pocket would be regarded as legal tender. He pondered this for some time, then pulled Ves aside. "Money," he whispered.

"Don't worry," Ves said. "I've got plenty."

"No," Swift said. "Don't you see? Our money no good here. Must get local money. How?"

"Why does everybody whisper in Pidgin?" Ves asked. "Why, for example, do you? Don't worry, I have some gold; that's money anywhere."

"What gold?"

"The coins from Brown, Lupoff & Gilden. I have the case in my pocket. Was going to return it to them this afternoon. We'll find some way to repay Mr. Gilden; right now, our need is greater than his."

Swift felt a twinge of custodial passion; a government agent does not lightly give up a valuable trust. Governments and banks are much alike in this regard. But Ves was right.

The tailor took his feet off the treadle, and the massive flywheel gradually slowed, the belts driving the gears lost their blur and slowed so their individual rubber teeth could be seen, and the ponderous, cranky sewing machine ground to a halt. "There's got to be some better way of doing this," the tailor said, glaring at his quarter-ton of gears, belts, flywheels, pulleys, cranks, eccentrics, and reciprocals that pushed the needle through the fabric and caught up the thread. "His Majesty's Government has spent how many millions on the dirigible? How many? 'First in lighter-than-air.' Transportation for the rich, that's what it is. That's what His Majesty's Government spends my tax money on. What about a little investment in perfecting the sewing machine? Have you ever been on a dirigible?"

"No," Ves admitted.

"Bah!" the tailor said, taking up his needle and starting the handwork. Then his eyes suddenly showed fright and he added, "Not that I'm complaining . . . No, not a word of complaint." He pointed to a small, rectangular sign on

the wall, bordered in black. It said: AMERICANS WORK
—THEY DON'T COMPLAIN. Ves and Swift looked at
the sign, then at each other.

"Say," Ves said, casually fingering a bolt of red and
green tweed, "what's the date?"

"The, ah, seventh, I think," the tailor said.

"Oh," Ves said.

"There's a *Times-Gazette* on the shelf under the counter," the tailor said. "May be the eighth."

"Ah!" Ves said. He went over to pick up the paper. It
was indeed the eighth: the eighth of September, 1897.
Wednesday. The *Times-Gazette* said so on the right side
of the masthead. On the left side it said: *A fair press
bodes no good man ill.*

Ves opened the paper and examined the front page. The
headline on the lead story, in a conservative pseudo-gothic
72-point type, announced: GOLD DISCOVERED IN
RUSSIAN AMERICA.

*Novye Alexanderobad 4 September, from our cor-
respondant.* RUMORS have reached the capital within the past few days of the discovery of a major
source of gold-bearing ore along the Yukon River in
the Klondike district of Russian America. The size of
the strike is not clear yet, but it is believed to be of
equal importance to the famous 1824 strike in Upper
California.

What the reaction to the news of Tsar Nicholas
will be is not yet known. Whether he will allow North
Americans to exploit the gold fields, or whether he
will close off the territory and bring in miners from
Russian Asia is the question of the day.

The expatriate American colony here is concerned
that a hardening of the Imperial policy toward casual
immigration might adversely affect the present American residents, many of whom are in self-imposed
political exile. Not a few of them are taking advantage of the difficulty of extradition proceedings
between Imperial Russia and the United States.

Any major influx of Americans to the border at
this time would present a particular problem to the
two governments. Some method of reassurance would
have to be arrived at to prevent a recurrence of the

unfortunate "false war" of two years ago, which was so unnecessarily destructive of lives and property.

A few of the other items on the front page were equally out of place in New York, in the 1897 Ves had been taught about. He pointed them out to Swift silently.

H D M RETURNS TO CAPITOL

HIS Democratic Majesty, Jacob Schuyler, by the Grace of God 11th President of the United States, brought his court back to Philadelphia yesterday. His Majesty will preside over the Joint Houses of Congress during the official opening ceremony on Monday the 13th. This will be the first time the Congress has sat since the ending of the famous Long Senate two years ago.

Article on Long Senate on page 8.

PRINCE MARTIN SIGHTED OVER SPHINX

THE *U.S.S. Prince Martin,* the largest lighter-than-air craft currently in operation in the World, has been reported passing over the Sphinx, a famous statue on the outskirts of the city of Cairo in Egypt.

The *Prince Martin,* commissioned two years ago July and named, with his Democratic Majesty's permission, after his eldest son, Martin, Prince of Texas, is now attempting to break the world's record for cruising non-stop around the World.

This epic flight was begun 27 days ago at Washington Naval Base in Virginia. The current World Record of 107 days was set in April-August, 1896 by the dirigible *Graf Ferdinand von Zeppelin,* under the able command of its builder Count Ferdinand von Zeppelin, and staffed by men and officers of the Balloon Command of the Prussian Army.

Continued on page 12

"We're somewhere else!" Swift said fervidly, dropping into one of the wooden chairs scattered around the shop.

"Tempora mutantur," Ves said softly.

"I mean, actually," Swift said. "It's like—it—it defies simile. I mean, entirely somewhere else. But we must have a common past somehow."

Ves nodded. "Post Revolutionary, I assume. We must

tread carefully in this strange water. We are unfamiliar with the mores, morals, religion, and politics of this place; let us be careful not to get stung. They seem more, ah, rigid here." He pointed to the cartoon on the editorial page of the *Times-Gazette*. It showed a large, heavily muscled man swinging a pick in the general direction of a railroad spike. The drawing was in a curious blocky, square style, and the caption read: "No time for play, AMERICA IS BEING BUILT BY THE SWEAT OF MY BROW."

"Your apparel, gentlemen," the tailor announced, coming out of his back room cubbyhole. "Is it the seventh?"

"No," Ves told him. "The eighth."

"Ah well," the tailor said, brandishing the two suits before him like shields. "One so loses track of time in the press of events." He seemed quite recovered from his attack of vexation over the monster sewing machine. "Try these on. I'll warrant they'll fit like new skin."

Ves and Swift put on their new suits, with the tailor hovering about them, fussing and fitting. When the three of them were satisfied with the garments' appearance, Ves took the flat coin case from the pocket of his old jacket. "How much do we owe you?" he asked.

"The suits with alterations are seven-fifty apiece," the tailor said. "I can allow you fifty cents apiece for the material from your old garments. That would make it fourteen dollars."

"You accept gold?"

The tailor stared at him. "You mean dust? Haven't seen any since I left Upper California ten years ago."

"Coins," Ves said. "Eagles d'or."

"Gold eagles? Gladly. Don't see many of them these days, either."

Ves produced the coins and handed the tailor two. The tailor stared at them, then looked suspiciously at Swift, then Ves. "Joke?" he said. "It's not funny, you know. I'm as loyal as the next man."

"Something wrong?" Ves asked.

"You sure you're foreigners?"

"Word of honor, we've never been here before in our lives."

"Where'd you get the coins?"

"They were given to us in a transaction."

"You know about Aaron Burr?"

"Who?" Ves asked.

"The gentleman whose picture's on the face of these coins. Aaron Burr."

"What about him?"

"He's a traitor. Was, I should say. President Hamilton had him tried for treason about eighty years ago, and he fled to Mexico. Hamilton sent the army in to hunt him down. That's how we ended up being at war with Spain and France, and an ally of Great Britain, so soon after fighting the Revolution. The War of 1814, we call it. Burr disappeared into Mexico."

"But that was"—Ves did some fast mental arithmetic—"eighty-three years ago. What has that got to do with our loyalty? Excuse our ignorance."

"There are a group of malcontents in this country," the tailor said, looking cautiously about as though he expected one of them to jump out from behind a rack of suits. "Jacobins, you know. They call themselves Burrites. They want a popular democracy—direct election of the President every four years. That sort of thing. You know what it says over the Hamilton Monument: 'The People are Turbulent and Changing.' No, of course you don't. Those are the Burrites: turbulent and changing. It is not respectable to talk about Aaron Burr. It is suspect. Alexander Hamilton never liked Aaron Burr. They almost fought a duel once. And to have a gold coin with Burr's face on it is unpatriotic. It's almost immoral. It's a peculiar thing to do for a prank."

"That's what we thought," Ves said. "But they can always be melted down. They *are* gold, after all."

"I'll think of something to do with them," the tailor said conspiratorially. "Here's your change."

TEN

"The New York Public Library," Ves said. "That's where I'll go. You'd be surprised how much of a private detective's investigating is done in a library. Of course, I doubt whether that beautiful building with the stone lions in front exists in this, ah, world; but they must have a library."

"What are we going to do in the library?" Swift asked. "I've never been very big on this esoteric research stuff. We have GS sevens for that. How's library research going to help us find the Constitution?" He and Ves were strolling leisurely up Madison Avenue, and had just reached the corner of Twenty-Seventh Street.

"We're looking for a pattern," Ves said, "and until we have enough of the pieces, we won't be able to see it. Until we have enough of the pieces, we won't even be able to tell for sure which are the right pieces. All we can do is collect pieces and try to fit them in. Eventually we'll be able to tell which pieces belong, and which don't."

"I wish I was taping that," Swift said. "I'd love to play it back to you."

"Besides," Ves said, "I believe in synchronicity."

"What does that mean?" Swift asked.

"It means if something happens, it was supposed to. All events have a direct cause and an effect—that's linear; but they all are also interrelated like a bunch of threads in a tapestry. We found this place, so we were supposed to come here. That being so, we won't merely be dropped off here, but will continue on. Whatever the story of the theft of the Constitution, we are now a part of it. Whether we will win or lose I cannot tell, but we will make an ending to the story, not just leave it in the middle."

"Is that what it means?" Swift asked. "That's a heavy load for one word to carry."

"That is what I believe," Ves said stiffly. "My personal philosophy, developed over a lifetime of watching events play themselves out. You'll see."

"If that's true," Swift said, "if some higher power is causing this sequence of events, why bother doing anything at all? Why not just check into some decent hotel and wait for events to catch up to us?"

"There *is* such a thing as free will," Ves said. "If we use our free will to opt out of the situation, then the situation will pass us by."

"All I can say about your philosphy is that I don't understand it," Swift said. "But then I don't understand Kant, Schopenhauer, Kahlil Gibran, Dylan, or Rod Mc-

Kuen, either. What I want now is to go to bed; a good fifteen hours' sleep. When I wake up, maybe I won't feel as if I was dreaming."

"You *have* been up for a while," Ves said. "Why don't we find a bed for you while I hunt up the library."

Lodging at the Gouverneur Morris, a plain but respectable hostelry on 34th Street and Fifth Avenue, across the street from where the Empire State Building stood in their world, cost thirty cents a night, bed and breakfast. Swift made use of the bed while Ves went off to discover the New York Public Library. The room clerk had located it for him at 42nd and Fifth—same place—and had assured him that it was open until ten p.m., "for the instruction and entertainment of shopgirls, and others who are unable to use the facilities during the day". When he returned at about ten-thirty, he didn't bother waking Swift, but merely collapsed in the next bed.

"What did you discover?" Swift asked him, over the prepaid breakfast the next morning.

"Same building, pretty much," Ves said. "You know the lions?"

"The ones out front?"

"Right."

"What about them?"

"Bison."

"What?"

"There's a pair of bison flanking the steps in this world. Very attractive, too. I spent my time reading history texts. High school stuff."

"What about it?" Swift asked, munching a hot biscuit.

"Everything's the same, far as I can tell, until about eighteen hundred. Who's the fourth president of the United States?"

"Let's see: Washington, Jefferson, ah, Adams, ah, Jackson . . . Jackson?"

"That's the advantage of being a naturalized citizen," Ves said. "You have to know all that stuff."

"I thought you were born in Baltimore," Swift said.

"I was, but my father was born in Carrara. He had to learn the names of all the presidents in order to get his papers. He thought that all Americans had to know the presidents, the amendments to the Constitution, all the states in alphabetical order, and all that sort of stuff. When he found out the school didn't make me memorize that stuff, *he* made me."

"Everybody learns that in school," Swift said.

"Name all the states in alphabetical order," Ves challenged. "I'll give you a hundred dollars if you get it right the first time; you give me five dollars a mistake. Debt payable on return to our own time—place—whatever."

"We'll have to try that sometime," Swift said, looking thoughtful. "What about the presidents?"

"Washington, Adams, Jefferson, Madison, Monroe, Adams (that's John Quincy), Jackson, van Buren, and now we're up to about 1840. That's the way I remember it."

"How do they remember it here?" Swift asked.

"That's the question. The litany here goes: Washington, Adams, Jefferson, Hamilton, Pinckney, Clinton, Schuyler, King—"

"Isn't there a Schuyler now?" Swift asked.

"Most of the names seem to repeat," Ves told him. "I would say that a small group of aristocrats have the Presidency all sewed up. They share it among themselves. I also think that if I said that in public, I'd be arrested. The presidency seems to be a figurehead office, but there's a lot of ceremony surrounding the figurehead, and one does not publicly insult him. Everything's more autocratic and repressed here. Have you noticed the signs?"

"What signs?"

Ves pointed to the wall, where a small framed sign showed an eye inset into the triangular tip of a pyramid, over the motto:

MINISTRY OF PUBLIC SAFETY
OUR EYES ARE EVERYWHERE
GUARDING YOUR RIGHTS

"Those signs are everywhere," Ves said.

"Swell," Swift said. "What else did you find out?"

"The Civil War," Ves said. "They didn't have one."

"No Civil War? What about slavery?"

"There was a big slave revolt in 1844, probably secretly backed by a group of Northern businessmen. It was crushed, and the surviving revoltees—is that a word?— were deported to Africa. I don't know whether slavery is practiced here now or not. If so, it would seem to be limited to the Southern states. New England doesn't need slavery, they have the Irish."

"Is that a crack?" Swift demanded.

"Don't be silly," Ves said. "I know you're Irish. There was a famine in Ireland a few years ago, and a couple of hundred thousand Irish came over here on indentures, and are now working in the mills. There are also a lot of Russians here, but the Tsar is not pleased."

"Then why did he let them go?"

"They tip-toe out. There's a big movement here to free the poor oppressed Russian peasants. It seems to be officially sanctioned. Relations between His Democratic Majesty and His Imperial Majesty are definitely strained."

Swift munched reflectively on a muffin. "His Democratic Majesty . . . It just doesn't sound right. We're in a parallel universe, you know? I read about that in a book once, but I thought they were kidding."

"They were," Ves said.

"The way I figure it," Swift said, waggling his spoon and splattering cocoa about the tablecloth, "there's *our* world, and there's *this* world, kind of side-by-side in the fourth dimension—or no, I guess it would be the fifth dimension—either they had parallel evolution, or they were the same until about eighteen hundred and then split apart."

"Then how come it's eighteen ninety-seven here?" Ves asked.

"How should I know," Swift explained.

"And what about the coins?"

"What coins?"

"The gold coins. Like the two I bought the suits with, or the one I've got right here"—he fished it out of his pocket. "Eagle d'or, it says. Mexico, it says. Aaron Burr, it says. Aaron Burr was never emperor of Mexico in this world. If there are parallel time tracks, there must be a whole bunch of them. Besides, if that character was *the* Alexander Hamilton, he died sixty years ago in this world."

Swift shrugged. "If there are two, why not twenty? Why not twenty thousand? As a matter of fact, if there are two, there are probably an infinity of them. Stretching out as far as the eye can see, if the eye could stand somewhere to watch. Somewhere Aaron Burr shoots Alexander

Hamilton, somewhere Alexander Hamilton shoots Aaron Burr, somewhere they both get it; somewhere they both miss, probably a few where one of the bullets ricochets and kills one of the seconds; somewhere the boat that takes them to Weehawken tips over, and one or both of them drown; somewhere Hamilton and Burr never met, somewhere they were lifelong friends. I could continue."

"Not with an audience," Ves said. "But I get your point. So where does that leave us?" He ticked off on his fingers: "One: there are an infinite number of parallel universes; two: a device exists to travel from one to another of these universes—or at least to a parallel Earth, we shouldn't be so cavalier with the word 'universe'— hidden in the wall of a steam room; three: there may be many more of these devices; four: Alexander Hamilton, for reasons of his own, is hunting for Aaron Burr among these parallel earths; five: someone has stolen the Constitution of the United States and left an almost exact duplicate in its place which; six: probably came from one of these alternate worlds and is a genuine Constitution."

"That would explain it," Swift agreed. "But how did he get it out of the vault?"

"How should I know?" Ves explained. "Find him and we'll ask."

"How?"

"Research. Find out about the entrances—these things in the walls—if there is more than one. Find out who set them up, who controls them, and who has access to them. Then find out the person from this group who has suddenly acquired a Constitution. Research and simple police work."

"Simple," Swift said. "And you're going to do this in the library?"

"It's a place to start," Ves said. "In the mass of public documents and newspapers will be the clue we need, if we know where to look."

"Where do we look?" Swift asked.

"I don't know yet," Ves admitted. "Finished with breakfast?"

Swift swallowed the last fragment of muffin and stood up. "I'll follow your lead, Ves," he said. "But you'll have to do the leading. I don't know anything about this kind of research. I wouldn't know what to look for if it bit me."

"I'll think of something," Ves promised.

The library was still closed when they got there: the sign on the door said eleven a.m., but the clock on the corner building across Fifth Avenue said five minutes past ten. "Better set our watches to local time," Swift said, pulling back his sleeve.

Ves grabbed his arm. "Cautiously!" he said. "We don't know whether wristwatches are in use here."

"Right." Swift did some subtle gyrations to hide his wrist from people while he reset the watch. "We have almost an hour. What shall we do with it?"

"Let's go over there," Ves said, indicating the corner building across the street. "There's an interesting shop on the Forty-Second Street side. At least the window looked fascinating at ten last night."

"I've noticed that," Swift said. "Shop windows always look infinitely more fascinating when the shops are closed."

They crossed Fifth and Forty-Second Street, dodging horse-drawn omnibuses, produce carts, heavy wagons, and hansom cabs, all of which seemed to have developed a maniacal desire to move through the traffic-lightless intersection in less time than the others. "Wow," Swift said, as he practiced deep breathing on the far corner, "never again will I yearn for the peaceful days before the automobile."

Santesson *Fils*, the store called itself. The window was a four-foot by four-foot square, and contained "Everything you have always coveted but seldom seen." There was an ancient astrolab with cabalistic symbols; a model Greek trireme with removable decks and tiny sailors manning the oars; a pair of huge brass binoculars with an identification plate in Turkic; a great headdress with many turkey and eagle feathers and a printed card saying: TO OUR BROTHER WALKS-SLOWLY-THROUGH-THE-RAIN, IN RECOGNITION OF HIS MANY SERVICES TO THE SIOUX NATION; a globe of some other world, mostly ocean; a large book, bound in leather, with an Arabic title and a locked flap across the front; a smaller book of architectural renderings of St. Augustine's *City of God;* the corpus of a small, prehensile mammal; a silver, castellated ring with a smoky green stone and a secret compartment; and a variety of intricate mechanisms of no apparent use.

The inside of the shop was small, jumbled, and even

stranger than the window. All available nooks, crannies, cubbyholes, and all flat surfaces were covered and filled with books. And on top of the books were piled books, upon which were balanced more books. Interspersed among the books were objects of strange and unique interest. There was a gadget that looked like a two-foot high ferris wheel, strung with buckets, levers, wires, and cogs, turning at a slow but steady rate. The plaque said: *PERPETUAL MOTION MECHANISM: PERFECTED BY Nathanial McCormick in 1856.*

There was a large, elaborate jar of the sort that the forty thieves hid themselves in (one to a jar). There was a box from which extended a mechanical arm, jointed to a mechanical hand, which held a pen. There was the proprietor: a medium-high, rather broad, unkempt man in his forties, jacketless, vest unbuttoned, sleeves rolled up, peering over a pamphlet at a desk in the rear of the room and ignoring his intruders with a majestic indifference.

"Hello," Ves called.

The man raised one arm without looking up from his pamphlet and waggled the hand.

"There is no such thing as perpetual motion," Swift said.

"E pur si muove," the unkempt man said, raising his gray eyes from the pamphlet to regard them for the first time. "It *does* move. Has for three years now. Although I'd be the first to admit that doesn't prove it's perpetual. What can I do for you gentlemen?"

"Just looking around," Ves said. "You have an intriguing shop."

"It intrigues me," the man admitted. "I've been everywhere and seen everything, and I've tried to bring a bit of each back with me. I make a living by trading off my memories, you might say."

"Everywhere?" Swift asked.

"Places you wouldn't believe," the man assured him.

"You'd be surprised what I'd believe," Swift said. Ves smiled a warning at him. The man either didn't notice, or wasn't impressed.

"I specialize in the smaller miracles," the man said. "Here, look at this." He took a tiny model of a coach and four from a shelf, and placed it on the only cleared table top in the store. No more than eight inches long, it was complete down to the finest detail that the eye could see:

four fine, brown horses in full harness pulling an elaborately embossed and gilded coach. The coachman, whip in hand, was seated in the driver's seat with two footmen in place in back.

Ves bent down to examine it. "Beautiful," he said. "The workmanship is exquisite. The painting detail on the figure is the best I've ever seen."

"Very nice," Swift said. "I'll bet if you like models, you'd be very impressed by it."

"It also moves," the man said. He touched a tiny stud on the top of the coach, and the horses sprang into motion. They raced around the table top, legs flashing, pulling the coach, while the coachmen guided them with reins and whip around in a tight circle. After three circuits of the table top, the coachman pulled the horses to a halt, and the coach stopped right where it had begun.

"Now *that*," Swift said, "is impressive!"

The tiny coachman dismounted and opened the coach door, and one of the footmen unfolded a two-step ladder from the door to the table top. A miniature lady in seventeenth-century court dress stepped out of the open door and down the two steps to the table. The coachman took her hand, she took three more steps away from the coach, gave a deep curtsey, and presented a letter she had been holding to the space between Swift and Ves. Then all motion ceased.

"Ah," Swift said, "um."

"It would have been more impressive," the man said, "if she had presented the letter directly to one of the two of you. My aim was slightly off."

"Clockwork?" Ves asked.

"That's right," the man said. "But that's like looking at a Rembrandt or a DeVacchio and asking 'paint?' " He carefully lifted the tiny coach and put it back on its shelf. "Keep looking around, gentlemen; if you see anything that interests you, call me." He nodded to them and returned to the close perusal of his pamphlet, at the desk in back of the store.

Ves noticed a rack of maps and started leafing through it. He had always been partial to maps; all sorts of maps. He collected maps. He had drawers full of maps. His prize, mounted under glass and hanging in his den, was a six-hundred-year-old chart of the island of Saaremaa (Osel), with a text laboriously hand-printed in Old Church

Vepse (or possibly Votyak). He had tried to have it authenticated and find out what it said, but there were only two men living in the United States who could read Old Church Vepse (or Votyak), and they worked for the Central Intelligence Agency and were not allowed to take outside work. The Museum of Ethnic Treasures in Tallin would probably claim it as a national treasure and complain officially to the State Department. And in the spirit of Detente, the State Department would probably trade his map to the Soviet government for a couple of sheep and a loaf of bread. So he would probably never know the names of the mountains of Saaremaa (Osel), or the depths of its inlets, or where the dragons were located.

The maps in this rack were various and interesting: a map of Africa with most of the interior marked *unknown,* and the Nile trailing off until it disappeared; a map of British America, with Ontario as its capital, which seemed to stretch farther south than Ves remembered; a humorously-drawn map of New York City, which showed Dutch burghers smoking their clay pipes on their plantations in Haarlam, merchants in bowlers waving at each other from their barges in Canal Street, the Mohawk Village in Central Park, and a busy ferry plying the wharfs between the independent cities of Brooklyn and New York.

Ves turned past the New York map, and was just starting to examine the next one, a nautical chart of Lake Huron, when he felt a sharp tapping at his shoulders. He spun around. "What—"

Swift had his finger to his lips. With his other hand he pointed to a glass case. Ves stared.

At first the contents made no sense, they were so varied and jumbled together. Then Ves's eye began to sort them out: a glass model of the Crystal Palace; a Malayan kris; a golden apple; a small glass cube with a swirl of stars imprisoned; a china Wellington; an old school tie; a model of the Great Pyramid, showing the Secret Burial Chamber and the Hidden Measurements; a brass model of the Empire State Building; an ivory model of a whale swallowing a ship . . .

"The Empire State Building?" Ves wondered aloud.

"That's what I thought it was," Nate said, "but it's good to have you agree. Should we ask the gentleman . . .?"

Ves shook his head. "I don't think so. We might watch

the shop, though. Or rather, you might. I'll continue my research. I'll be right across the street, between the famous stone bison, if you need me."

Swift and Ves casually left the shop. "You want *me* to watch him," Swift said. "Why not, I've got nothing else to do. He probably lives in the back of the shop. I'll just lounge inconspicuously by that lamp post across the street. You might remember to bring me a sandwich once or twice a day; if they've invented the sandwich here."

"If you need me," Ves told Swift, "you can always call me on your button, and I'll come right down. If we had any money, I'd attempt to hire a couple of private inquiry agents to help, but we're down to our last gold coin."

"You know, there's an idea," Swift said. "Why don't I just go back to the device and return to our own world —or time—or whatever, to get money and help? I'll be back in a couple of hours at most."

"What do we do if you're not back?" Ves asked. "Suppose that contraption only sends in one direction, and you end up further in the past? Or, suppose you don't work the controls right and end up nowhere at all? What would I do then?"

Swift considered. "On balance, you're right," he decided. "I'd hate to disappear and leave you in trouble. As a matter of fact, I'd hate to disappear."

Ves left Swift loitering across the street and went up to the library's current periodical room, about two steps behind the newly-arriving librarian. He pulled the past two months' files of New York's three largest daily papers: the *Times-Gazette*, which seemed to concentrate on international and political news; the *World*, which was mostly local news; and the *Tattler*, which did. The librarian, a prim lady who looked as though she ought to be wearing glasses but didn't, took a strong interest in either Ves or his research, he couldn't tell which, and insisted upon being helpful.

"I keep very current," she told him. "What *are* you researching? It must be frightfully interesting! I should be glad to assist you; it's no more than my duty."

Ves decided that taking her up on her offer would be the easiest way to keep her quiet. "I'm looking for unusual events," he told her. "Anything really strange or out of the ordinary; anything unexplained or unexplainable, might be what I'm looking for. I can't explain it better than that."

"I know *just* what you mean!" she told him. "Let me look through some of the journals."

Ves continued his research, making notes with a library pencil on library-supplied scratch paper of anything that caught his fancy, that might prove to be part of the pattern. Of course, it was hard to tell what was usual in this world from what was unique. The naked man caught running through the streets of Brooklyn last Sunday night for example; was he a traveller who had departed some other steam bath in greater *déshabillé* than they, or was he a harmless, uninteresting drunk? The newspaper report gave no indication, and they might just have to look him up to find out. Or the strange and sudden disappearance of a ship, loaded with Madeira wine, from its pier on Pier Street; was that a case of clever piracy, of sudden sinking, or was Madeira bringing a premium price in some other dimensional wine market? He'd probably never know.

"Here's something that might interest you," the librarian said, thrusting an open magazine in front of him. FRENCH PROFESSOR PROPOSES FIRING ROCKET TO MOON, the article was entitled. The picture, across the top halves of both pages, showed a large bullet-like projectile with rivets all over it and a window in the side. Two men were peering out of the window at the moon, which had a face arranged in a grotesque wink. Smoke was coming out of the back of the projectile.

"Fascinating," Ves said, staring in open admiration at the picture.

"You said anything strange," the librarian said. "Now *that's* pretty strange. Like that New Jersey man who claims he can send messages through the air by magnetism. It always amazes me how gullible people are."

"Ves," Swift's voice sounded in his ear, *"Hamilton just went into that shop."*

Ves touched the button. "Keep your eye on them."

"Of course. You might consider getting down here."

"What's that?" the librarian demanded. "Whom?"

"Right away," Ves said into the button, getting up.

"Now?" The librarian sounded shocked. "But I hardly know you!"

Ves took the librarian's hand. "Thank you very much

for your help," he said. "I must leave now, but I shall return. Perhaps we shall get to know each other better then. *Adieu!*" He strode through the door and down the wide marble stairs to the main hall.

"Ves! He's come out again. Headed north. I'm going to follow."

Ves touched the button. "Right. I'll be right behind you."

Two large men in very plain clothes and bowler hats detached themselves from separate marble pillars by the doors and approached Ves. "May we speak to you for a second?" the one on the left asked, politely tipping his hat.

Ves stopped and spread his arms. "Search me," he said. "Nary a book concealed on my person."

"We don't work for the library," the one on the right said.

"Was this yours?" the one on the left inquired, producing a gold coin from his pocket.

Ves unobtrusively touched the button. "I may be awhile," he murmured into it.

"That's true," the man on the left said.

ELEVEN

||||||||||||||||||||||||||||||

Swift was prepared for a long wait. No, that's not true: Swift was expecting a long wait, but he wasn't prepared for it. He was dreading it. He had no idea of what he was looking for, or how to recognize it when it came. "Anything out of the ordinary," Ves had said. Swift pictured a parade of centaurs and unicorns coming out of the shop with Empire State buildings and Statues of Liberty tied to their backs.

The shop did not seem to be overly popular. Many people passing by paused to look in the window, but none of them entered the door. Swift was getting bored. The only man to enter the store didn't pause at the window first, and it was only after he had gone in that Swift realized it was Alex: Hamilton himself. Swift called Ves, but before Ves could join him Hamilton had left the store and was heading north on Fifth Avenue. Swift decided to follow Hamilton, since the store would stay where it was. Besides, Hamilton had started all this. Unless it was Aaron Burr.

Ves said he would be right behind. Then: *"I may be awhile,"* and nothing more. Swift didn't have time to consider that; he was loping along behind the fastest broken-sidewalk pacer on Fifth Avenue. Alex: didn't sneak about; he strode with majestic unconcern for those who bobbed in his wake.

Hamilton carried a small package, wrapped in brown paper, under his arm. Swift didn't think he had seen it before Hamilton entered the shop; therefore he had picked it up in the shop. Deductive reasoning: QED: elementary, my dear Ves. Swift amused himself as he scurried along, trying to decide which of the many objects he had seen in the shop was now under Hamilton's arm.

Alex: Hamilton strode from Forty-Second to Eighty-Third Street, slightly over two miles, without pausing or breaking his stride. The Prussian Army would have been proud, had he been one of theirs. He entered the main doors of the Metropolitan Chartered Museum of Arts and Crafts, with Swift half a block behind.

Swift climbed the stairs to the museum and paused to take breath. Once he had stopped, he found that he had a lot of breaths to take. "Is this the only exit?" he asked a uniformed guard at the head of the stairs.

"Exit and entrance," the guard told him. "Turnstile right through the doors."

"Thank you," Swift said, still breathing hard. He pushed through the fifteen-foot high bronze doors and looked around. The hall was vast, three stories high, and faced in white marble. Massive skylights brought the daylight in, while giant chandeliers hung from the marble ceiling to provide light at dusk. The areas that were not lit directly by the skylight were cast into deep shadow, a *chiaroscuro* effect which was heightened by the stark whiteness of the marble. Seven arched corridors led off the main hall, disappearing into gloom within a few feet.

"Where did he go?" Swift demanded of the attendant at the turnstile.

"Fifty cents donation, sir," the attendant said, nodding.

"The gentleman who came in a half-minute ago," Swift said, "which way did he go?"

"Off to the left, sir. Either into 'Teapots of the World', or the Toltec-Aztec-Hebrew-Phoenician wing, I am not positive which."

"The Toltec-Aztec-Phoenician wing?"

"Toltec-Aztec-Hebrew-Phoenician, sir. A gift of Sir Dandridge Phillipotts, right after he proved that the American Indians are the ten lost tribes of Israel, sir. Fifty cents donation, sir."

"Oh, yes." Swift patted his pocket, then realized. "I don't have anything you would consider money. Not with me."

"Very good, sir," the attendant said. "Here,"—he lifted a ledger that was chained to the post and set it on the table—"sign the pauper's book. One of our benefactors will make up your donation. *Pro bomo publico,* sir."

It wasn't merely a signature that was wanted, but more of a dossier. The headings went across both pages: *Name, address, occupation, religion, sex, political affiliation, nationality, reason for using museum.* With the horrible feeling that Alex: Hamilton was getting farther and farther into 'Teapots of the World', Swift made up answers at random and wrote them in. "Here you are," he said, spinning the book around, "and thank you."

The attendant stared down at the book. *Name:* Octavius Caesar; *Address:* usually 'Augustus' or 'Principus'; *occupation:* most of Mediterranean; *Religion:* Pantheistic Paganism; *Sex:* God; *Political Affiliation:* Mystic Workers Party; *Nationality:* Dyspeptic; *Reason for Using Museum:* Lack of public facility on street. "Very good, sir. That seems very complete, sir. Just step through the turnstile."

Swift quickly looked over the "Teapots of the World" collection, which was deserted, and then entered the Toltec-Aztec-Hebrew-Phoenician wing. It was a long corridor with rooms off both sides. Some of the rooms held display cases full of artifacts, and others contained representations of scenes in the history of the Ten Lost Tribes. None of the rooms that Swift passed were occupied by so much as a museum guard. Swift touched the button on his communicator and called, "Ves, do you hear me?" His voice reverberated through the corridor, but there was no answer. "Ves," he whispered into the button, "where are you?"

"Why are you following me, young man?"

Swift looked up. Alex: was standing in the doorway to one of the side rooms, staring at Swift down his patrician nose.

Swift thought of several possible answers, but none seemed suitable. "Following you?" he asked.

"It really doesn't matter," Alex: said. "If you want to follow me, then do so. Come along." He turned and strode into the room.

The plaque at the door said "RECREATION OF IN-TERIOR OF AZTEC TEMPLE: SACRIFICIAL ROOM designed by Professor J. Leavett." The interior was dominated by a great, round, flat-top stone, covered with intricate carving. It was lit by flickering gaslights coming out of artificial torches, set into the pseudo-stone walls. Through the small stone windows could be seen painted scenes of a great Aztec city spread out below the temple. The atmosphere was murky, ancient, and oppressive. Swift paused at the door.

"Well, come on if you're coming," Alex: said, climbing up onto the sacrificial stone and smoothing the crease in his trousers. He stooped and opened a latch concealed in the stone slab.

"Where are you going?" Swift asked, climbing up after Alex:.

"A little late to ask that, isn't it?" Alex: said, reaching into the stone and pushing a button.

TWELVE

||||||||||||||||||||||||||||

Ves was willing to explain his possession of the gold coin to the two officers. He was eager to explain. He had always been proud of his ability to talk his way out of anything: an ability that a private detective quickly acquires if he wishes to stay in business and keep all his teeth. The only trouble was, the officers wouldn't let him explain. They weren't interested in anything he had to say. They refused to listen to him. Their only interest was in fastening the large, old-fashioned handcuffs around his wrists and leading him away from the library.

The first part proved to be something of a problem. These handcuffs didn't work with a key, they screwed closed with a great plug screw, which refused to turn.

"You've got it mis-threaded; here, let me," said One.

"There's some mistake, gentlemen," said Ves.

"No mistake, you've let the cuffs get rusty," said Two.

"I'm sure I can explain to your satisfaction," Ves said.

"I keep 'em greased proper," said One.

"Them threads are tiny," Two said. "One little speck of rust can screw up the works. Or, I should say, can't."

"I came across the coin by accident," Ves said. "Perhaps I could lead you gentlemen to the person who passed it on to me? A stout man with a broad moustache. I'm sure I'd know him."

"Just keep holding your hands behind you till we get these cuffs on you," One said.

"I don't want to cause you trouble," Ves said, wishing he could reach the communicator button with his teeth. "This is all some mistake."

"There it goes," said Two. "I got it screwing in."

"Think you'll be able to get them off?" asked One.

"What difference?" demanded Two. "Can't take a prisoner in without gyves; it isn't done. Can always cut them off, once he's in."

"True," said One.

"If you gentlemen would just tell me what you want . . ." said Ves.

"Come along now," said One, taking him firmly by the upper arm. "We'll be at Central Office in no time."

"Central Office?" Ves asked.

"Do we look like we're out of the local precinct?" Two asked, sounding slightly insulted.

"No," Ves said. "Of course not."

"No time" was slightly under an hour. It would have been less, but the traffic on Fifth Avenue was very heavy, or so Two said when they reached Eighth Street. It was the first thing he'd said since they enfered the carriage, being preoccupied with 'Looking Stern and Staying Alert' in case Ves tried anything desperate. One was up with the driver and the door was locked from the outside, but better safe than sorry, as One had said when locking the door.

They turned right on Eighth Street, went over to Sixth Avenue, turned back downtown and went several more blocks; they pulled up at a high, long, brick wall with one gate, closed by a massive iron door. The driver yelled, the gate opened, and the people on the street stood respectfully by with their hats off while the carriage drove in and the gate slammed behind it. That gesture, more than anything else, made Ves nervous.

The brick wall enclosed a large courtyard fronting a three-story brick building, with very severe lines. The windows were small and barred with wrist-thick iron bars on all three floors. The only visible door was massive and banded in steel. The square white sign with neat black lettering to the left of the door said:

MINISTRY OF PUBLIC SAFETY
INTERNAL SECURITY
NORTHEAST DIVISION
PUBLIC SAFETY IS A PUBLIC TRUST

all citizens subject to search beyond this point

The carriage pulled right up to the door, and One hopped down and opened the door. Ves got out and, flanked by One and Two, walked to the door. It was opened from the inside by a uniformed guard, who peered at them through a peephole before pulling the latch. Ves was led upstairs one flight to a small room with a number on the door, seated on a wooden bench, and left there.

By twisting his neck, Ves managed to get the collar of his jacket between his teeth. He chewed steadily toward the pin holding the transmitter button. When he finally got hold of it, he mouthed, "Nate, Nate, this is Ves", between his clenched teeth. Then he realized how silly that was: who else could it be? There was no answer. Well, the range of the tiny button transmitters was no more than a kilometer at best; Swift had been walking north, and he had been driven south. Ves gave up on chewing his collar and settled down to wait.

They kept him waiting for quite a while. It would have bothered him if he weren't quite familiar with the technique, having used it himself to break down suspects. The longer they wait, the more nervous they get, the more chance they have to think—and they can only think of their crime—the more eager they are to tell you about it; even if it's only to deny that it ever happened. He had often found out about frauds his employer never suspected, by having someone he was questioning deny committing them.

After what his interrogators thought was a sufficient pause, they had him brought into the office next to his waiting room. They had all the customs and style going for them, and showed signs of vast experience. The only thing missing was the bright light, but their technology wasn't quite up to it.

There were three of them in the room: one behind a giant desk to sneer at him, another one to loom over him, and one to sit quietly in a corner and be on his side: the "friend" he would eventually confess to, if the pressure didn't break him first.

They took the handcuffs off and emptied his pockets: wallet, keychain, coins, the remaining gold coin in its case, magnifying glass, vestpocket microscope, felt-tip pen, small flip-top notebook, two-bladed penknife. The one behind the desk took the wallet, removed the papers from it one at a time, studied them closely, and then passed them around. They were very popular, almost every one eliciting at least a smile from each of the inquisitors. His drivers license was quite popular, and brought forth a chuckle from the man behind the desk, while the man in the corner shook his head sadly and knowingly.

Finally the man behind the desk looked up at Ves. "Sit down," he ordered.

"Thank you," Ves said, sitting down.

"You may call me Colonel Brown," the man behind the desk said. "This is Captain Lewis and Captain Richardson," he indicated the loomer and the corner sitter.

"My name is Romero," Ves said. "It's good of you to see me like this. I'll try not to waste too much of your time."

Colonel Brown looked vaguely puzzled; this was the wrong reaction. He continued, "Your master never stops trying, does he? And you people never can get anything right."

"Excuse me?" Ves asked.

Colonel Brown chuckled mildly. "Oh, come now," he said. "Do you take us for fools?"

"On the contrary, Colonel Brown," Ves said. "Would I have wanted to see you if I didn't have a high regard for your intelligence?"

"You wanted to—Lewis, come here!" He stood up abruptly and walked to the door, with Captain Lewis at his heels. Colonel Brown stalked through, and was about to slam the door when he paused and turned. "Ah, excuse us for a second." The door closed softly behind him. Captain Richardson, left sitting in the corner, smiled and fidgeted, and didn't try to make conversation. Ves practiced deep breathing exercises and thinking good thoughts to stay relaxed; any tenseness inside his body in the immediate future could only work against him, and he needed every edge he could get.

About five minutes went by before the Colonel and Captain Lewis returned. They had formulated their plans and decided to attack. "What did you mean," the Colonel demanded, "you wanted to see me? *I* sent for *you*, didn't I?"

Ves looked up mildly. "Then I suppose we wanted to see each other," he said. "Didn't your men tell you?"

"Well," the Colonel leaned back in his chair and laced his fingers together. "Let's get to my questions first, then we'll consider yours. I admit I'm curious. But now tell me: to whom do you report and who are your agents in New York?"

"I think we'd better do this the other way around," Ves said. "Your assumptions are based on a false premise."

Captain Lewis leaned forward and grabbed Ves by the collar. "The Colonel don't like to be talked to that way," he said.

"You know, what gives you Russians away is always the same thing," the Colonel said. "Lack of attention to detail. Let go of him, Captain."

"I'm Italian-American," Ves said, smoothing his collar and leaning back in the chair.

"What do you mean?" the Colonel asked. "Lombardy? Tuscany? Rome? Piedmont? You trying to tell me you owe allegiance to the Austrian Empire instead of the Russians?

Give us a list of the Austrian agents working in the United States."

"You don't understand," Ves said.

Captain Lewis grabbed his collar again. "Just answer the—ow!—what the hell is that?" He let go of the collar and thrust an injured finger into his mouth. "You've got a pin in your coat!" he said accusingly.

"I'm sorry," Ves said. "Here, let me . . ." He removed the pin and dropped it into his pocket. "You people seem to think I'm a Russian spy," he said. "Some things never change. Although we're bigger on the Chinese than the Russians right now."

"What's that about China?" the Colonel demanded.

"Listen," Ves said. "I'm from somewhere else; another place, another time: somewhere quite different from here. To me, this is the past, only it isn't because it's different—changed. But I'm not a Russian, Lombardian, Chinese, Austrian, or Swiss. I'm a visitor from a different universe."

"With forged papers?" the Colonel asked, unimpressed.

"They're not forged," Ves insisted.

"These documents are not only false, they're ludicrous," the Colonel said. "That's why we think you're Russian; Tsar Nicholas is not a fiend for accuracy, and the Cheka tends to be very slipshod about English-language forgery. But we're ready to believe you're Austrian, if you want to admit you're Austrian. Convince us that you're Austrian."

"I don't even speak Austrian—or Russian either, for that matter," Ves said.

"A negative is the hardest thing to prove," the Colonel said.

"I am from somewhere else," Ves said. "I am a visitor to your world. Just passing through, you might say. I am not any sort of spy."

"What are you doing here?" the Colonel asked.

"We seek a man from our world who is thought to have stolen something of great importance."

" 'We,' " the Colonel said. "You and your companion. We know of him. Where is he?"

"I don't know," Ves said. "He was following the suspect."

"It would go easier with you if you'd talk," Captain Richardson spoke up from the corner. "I'd like to help you."

"I've heard enough of this bull," Captain Lewis said,

giving his best imitation of a savage sneer. "Just leave me alone with him for a few minutes; I'll find out everything he knows!"

"I'm sure you could, Captain," Colonel Brown said.

"You looked at the documents in my wallet," Ves said. "Did you notice the dates on them? Take a look at my drivers license—the one with my picture on it—the date's on top."

"You insist upon this ridiculous story?"

"How do you explain the license?" Ves demanded.

The Colonel stared at it for a long time, turning it over and over in his hand. "Forgery," he said finally.

"Why would anyone forge a non-existent document?" Ves asked. "None of those cards or papers correspond to any that you use here."

The Colonel nodded. "That's just it," he said. "If you were from the future, you'd be well supplied with genuine documents to copy; but if you were from *Russia,* then you'd have to improvise. This might all be a clever ruse," he added, waving at the assorted papers. "A big lie to tell, if you're questioned."

"What would be the point to that?" Ves asked.

"Aha!" the Colonel said. "What indeed, that's the question. And don't think that we won't find the answer. Now, what's the purpose of those gold coins?"

"Purpose?" Ves asked.

"Don't get wise," Captain Lewis shouted, his mouth three inches from Ves's ear. "Answer the Colonel!"

"Who were you to distribute them to? How many more are there? What do the Burrites plan to do with them?"

"I wasn't distributing them to anyone in particular," Ves said. "I was only using them for their gold value because they happened to be in my pocket. There are no more, as far as I know; and to the best of my knowledge, I've never met a Burrite."

The Colonel stood up, anger evident in the set of his chin, the flash of his eye, and the color of his ears. "I've had about enough of this," he said, slapping his palm down on the desk with a resounding *thwack!* "There are certain questions I want answers to. We'll play your little game after, if you like, but right now we'll play mine. Captain Lewis, come outside for a moment."

Colonel Brown strode through the door, the captain at his heels. Captain Lewis turned around in the doorway.

"I'll be back," he said, cracking his knuckles suggestively. "Be patient a minute longer, oh visitor from the future. I'll be back—and we'll talk." With this gentle threat, he slammed the door.

Ves sat there staring at the door. Captain Richardson stayed quietly in the corner. *Now it comes,* Ves thought. *Rough and smooth. Lewis has threatened. Now Richardson will try to save me, and I'll feel grateful and tell him all. I wish I could think of something clever to say: they obviously won't believe the truth.*

"I'd like to help you," Richardson said softly from his corner seat.

Hahaha, Ves thought.

"I think there's something I can do, if you'll help," Richardson said.

"What's that?" Ves asked, playing along.

"I think I can get you out of here," Richardson said. He patted his jacket pocket. "Would you like a cigar? I'd offer you a cigarette, but they haven't been invented here yet."

Ves looked at him for a minute, speechless. "You don't say," he said, finally. "I mean, what did you say?"

"I'm Prime," Captain Richardson told him. "I'm here on a mission for the Directory. What are you doing here —and why the ridiculous mix-up in the paperwork?"

"It's no mix-up," Ves said. "That's my real driver's license, social security card and stuff. I'm from nineteen ninety-six. A nineteen ninety-six where the fourth President of the United States had been Madison, not Hamilton."

"Ah," Captain Richardson said, "*That* nineteen ninety-six." He chuckled softly.

"What do you find so funny?" Ves demanded.

"It's just that you don't understand the immensity of the random-space cycle. It's infinite. And any slice of it, for all practical purposes, is also infinite."

"What does that mean?" Ves asked, afraid he knew.

"It means that there are an infinite number of times where the fourth president of the United States was James Madison. They are all sandwiched in between Hamilton and, I believe, a third term for Jefferson. Just as there are an infinite number of fractions sandwiched in between one-fourth and one-half."

"Does that mean you can get me back home?"

"Oh, of course not. Luckily we can only reach certain of these infinite worlds; and though there are a great many of them, they are spread far enough apart in time to make them easily recognizable. Just keep track of what time it is in your home world."

"Fair enough. How are you going to get me out of here?"

"If you're not from Prime, I should just let you rot," Captain Richardson said cheerfully. "It'll take considerable trouble and effort to get you to an It. But, I suppose, it must be considered in its humanitarian aspect. I mean, to leave you in the hands of these barbarians . . ."

"An It?" Ves interrupted.

"Yes, yes. An It. An I.T. An Intertemporal Translator. As in: Translate, *v*, to bear, convey, or remove from one person, place, or condition to another. For example: 'It was his opinion that when he died he would be instantly translated to Heaven, but for my part, I think the Devil read him better.' And: Intertemporal, *adj.*, between the times. For example: 'Intertemporal night is a lonely place, but a place where a man can feel free. You don't feel like part of—' Why are you staring at me that way?"

Ves shook his head. "I don't know. Suddenly it all seemed too much. What's going to happen?"

"Only the dinosaurs know that," Captain Richardson said. "Just follow my lead and I'll take care of you. Someone will be in touch with you later. The password is, um, something from our common history would be nice. I have a sense of the fitness of things, a feeling of Kismet, of karma; and since the Universe so seldom goes along with human notions of what is predestined, we should encourage it in every way. You're staring again. Do you find it strange to wish to encourage the Universe? But what else can we do? I, for one, would not like to attempt to discourage the Universe; it might decide to discourage *me*. *Kismet!* That's the very word! Kismet it is, and I wish you good karma."

Ves shrugged, a shrug that came from his soul and his Trentino-Alto Adigean ancestors. "Much obliged," he said.

Captain Richardson glanced at the door and got busy. "Here," he said, thrusting a cigar at Ves, "stick this in your mouth. Puff on it a bit. We're supposed to be making friends, and I'm softening you up to talk. I *do* have my position here to consider, you know." He struck a sulfurous match and applied the flame to the cigar tip. "If you're the dumb sort of clod who inhales tobacco smoke, refrain from inhaling the first few drags of this. That match will cleanse your lungs out of your body."

"Tell me," Ves said, "what do you do here? I mean, why are you here?"

"Well," Captain Richardson said. "I'm a temporalist; a sort of anthropologist-sociologist. I study primitive cultures by living and taking part in them. Someday we hope to be able to control our own by what we learn here."

"What have you learned?" Ves asked.

"Well," Captain Richardson puffed on his cigar. "Let me put it this way: the three guiding words of the temporalist philosophy, gained after two hundred years of doing this sort of thing, are: 'leave it alone'. And it took us a hundred and fifty years to learn that. Some of us . . ." he paused and listened for a second . . . "Of course, I am your friend. You must understand that Colonel Brown has a job to do. If you help him, I'm sure he will help you. A new job, a new identity, somewhere where the Cheka can't find you. Ah, Colonel—our friend here has agreed to talk. No need for Captain Lewis and his French Persuasion."

THIRTEEN

Nothing seemed to have changed, but suddenly the room smelled bad. The torches were now flickering and giving off an aura of thick black smoke. The perspective through the windows was different. Swift revised his first opinion, and decided that much had changed. "What happened?" he asked.

"That's almost as silly as 'Where am I?'," Alex: commented, closing the little hatch in the stone.

"That was going to be my next question," Swift assured him, climbing down from the stone slab. "Along with 'what the hell is going on here', 'what do you think you're doing', and 'why are those naked men with knives coming through the door'?" With the last question, Swift circled around the stone to keep its bulk between himself and the three naked men with knives who had just come through the door.

"They are not naked," Hamilton said indignantly. "They wear breechclouts and feather headdresses, the proper attire for persons in service here in Tehetiltotipec. I would certainly never allow any persons of mine to go around naked. Even the women wear proper dresses. Although I'll admit that some of the natives back in the hills. . . Oh, well; civilization moves slowly in its progress."

"These Indians are in your service?" Swift asked, ceasing to crouch behind the stone slab.

"Certainly," Hamilton affirmed. "Well, ah, to be technical about it; actually they think I'm some sort of a god. They work much cheaper if they think you're a god."

"Why do they think that?" Swift asked.

"Well, you know, it's because I told them I was, that's why." Hamilton looked embarrassed.

"You *told* them you were a god?" Swift asked, the astonishment evident in his voice.

"Yes. Well, I suppose I could have told them about Jehovah, Original Sin, Purgatory, the Elect, and all that; but I didn't think it would do either of us much good. Since all of the Elect live in Boston, and this is on the other coast, I didn't think they'd appreciate that particularly overmuch."

"You're probably right," Swift said. "The *other* coast?"

"You're a slow learner, aren't you son," Hamilton said kindly. "That's right. This is the city of Tehetiltotipec. On other levels known as Mission Dolores, or Yerba Buena, or Drake's Bay, or San Francisco. Come along with me now, and tell me why you've been following me."

They went out into the sunlight, and from the top of the ziggurat, which perched on a hill, highest of a series of hills, Nate Swift could see the city of Tehetiltotipec spread out beneath him. The sun, halfway down to the western sea, spread lengthening shadows over the small, closely-packed brick buildings and the narrow, twisting streets. *Nob Hill?* Swift wondered. He wasn't sure enough of the basic shape of San Francisco Peninsula, without its tall downtown buildings, to be sure just where the great stepped pyramid had been built. Off to the north Alcatraz

Island shone green, golden and white, with some sort of high wall surrounding it, and low buildings visible within the walls. Swift pointed it out to Hamilton. "A prison again?" he asked.

"Prison? No, that's the Treasury of the Iztahatitipec Empire." Hamilton led Swift down the staircase running down the center of one side of the tall ziggurat. At the bottom, in the dirt street, a four-man palanquin awaited. Hamilton mounted and motioned to Swift to join him. "It will hold two," he said. "The bearers change frequently and are used to the load."

Swift climbed in beside Hamilton, and the bearers dog-trotted down the street. They tried to keep in step, but the ride was as rough above as it was heavy below. "Thank you," Swift said, "I think."

"Now," Hamilton said, "I am a very patient man. All of my colleagues will tell you that I am a very patient man. But even a patient man—a very patient man—has his limits. Why have you been following me?"

"Tell me," Swift said, "are you the real Alexander Hamilton?"

"I live, I breathe, I spit, I am," Hamilton said. "And I am the only Alexander Hamilton I know of. There are, of course, the innumerable doppelgangers in each of the time tracks where I was born. (Doubles-ganger?). But each of them—of us—is as real an Alexander Hamilton as any of the others. Our language is not prepared for the problems of parallel times. I am intimately concerned with the needs of the Alexander Hamilton confined in this body, although I intellectually recognize the identity of all Alexander Hamiltons. Does this in any way answer your question?"

"Let's try this," Swift said: "Are you the Alexander Hamilton who signed the Constitution of the United States?"

"I am he," Alexander Hamilton said. He leaned back and looked satisfied. "That I shall always be."

Swift decided not to mention the alternate version of the Constitution, or who had signed it. They rode together in silence for a while, then stopped, tipped forward, and were put down.

"We have, I assume, arrived," Hamilton said.

"Where?" Swift asked, climbing out of the palanquin and looking about. They were on a wooden jetty sticking out into the bay. Pulled up alongside the pier was a fat bireme; the prow, in the shape of an angry alligator, snapping its teeth at the sea waves. Two double-banks of naked, oiled rowers waited silently, with shipped oars, for the steady drumbeat to begin.

"The ferry," Hamilton said, indicating the craft with a wave of his aristocratic hand. "How is it that I seem to be answering all of your questions, while you are avoiding my only one?"

"Ferry?" Swift asked.

Alexander Hamilton sighed. "Come along," he said. "I wouldn't want you to have to swim after the boat. We cross the bay to Xantitipetal—Oakland in your world—and the Intercontinental Coach."

"The Intercontinental Coach?"

"Just come along," Hamilton said. "Living it is so much easier than explaining it. And while we're en route, perhaps you will tell me something of yourself; like why you're following me."

They traversed the narrow gangplank onto the ferry, and followed the roped walk to the passenger deck at the rear. The ropes were cast off, and the warning beat of the drum started the oarsmen on their steady task. Nate Swift found himself fascinated by the rhythmic consort of the oarsmen, and the sullen expressions on their faces.

"Why are you so fascinated by the rowers?" Hamilton asked.

"I was wondering if they have a good union," Swift told him.

"They are convicts," Hamilton said. "Guilty of crimes from unorthodoxy to murder. They get three days off their sentence for every day on the galley. Now sit down and enjoy the trip."

Swift sat down and tried to relax, but he felt as though he had just been told that the black powder in the barrel was cordite; now sit down on it and enjoy your smoke. "Forced labor always makes me nervous," he said.

"One of the results of progressive Democracy," Hamilton said scornfully. "The great leveling process, until finally anyone who is superior is afraid to stick his head above the herd. Remember, my boy, the laboring classes were made to labor; do not try to make them think, it only makes them irritable and angry."

Swift stared at him, amazed. "I thought you were a Democrat."

"You thought *what?*" It was Hamilton's turn to be amazed. "I'm a Federalist."

"I didn't mean political party," Swift said. "I meant, I thought you were in favor of popular democracy."

"I never was," Hamilton said. "Never. Is *that* what they taught you?"

"Well, you signed the Constitution; you were one of the heroes of the Revolution . . ."

"Just because I objected to the methods of George the Third, that bumbling idiot, doesn't mean I'm opposed to the principle of monarchy. Jefferson believes in the natural aristocracy of the Noble Farmer. Pah! Jefferson has never met any farmers. He thinks he's a farmer because he owns several thousand acres of land at Monticello and his slaves grow things on it. Washington believes in the natural aristocracy of himself."

"You think some people are better than others? Some people are naturally fit to govern, while others should only serve? Some kind of a genetic split between master and servant?"

"Not at all," Hamilton said. "I believe in the natural baseness of Man. But the uneducated are too short-sighted to even know what their own self-interest is, and can be led by any knave with a golden voice. Burr is very popular with the masses. The educated have a better chance of seeing through the simpler sorts of deceit, and the rich or well-born are more able to resist the blandishments of the cruder sorts of bribery."

"Which is why these poor brutes should spend their lives rowing back and forth between Oakland and San Francisco?"

"Xantitipetal and Tehetiltotipec," Hamilton said absently. "No, not at all. But, whereas I can take advantage of this primitive Empire, it is quite beyond my ability to do anything to change it."

"I thought you were a god," Swift said.

"True," Hamilton said. "Do you realize just how circumspect a god has to be? It's all right to appear now and again and go about my mysterious godlike errands; but if I start expounding beliefs contrary to their dogma, the priests will quickly remember that even gods are mortal."

"I never realized what a heavy load it was to be a god," Swift said, shaking his head.

"But now to you," Hamilton said, "and your philosophy of life."

"You mean, why was I following you," Swift said.

"Exactly," Hamilton said. "You have a quick and incisive wit. Why?"

"It's a long story," Swift said, "and it started with the Constitution of the United States." And he went on explaining to Hamilton what had happened. "I had some doubts about telling you," he said in conclusion. "But it suddenly occured to me that if I can't tell Alexander Hamilton what happened to the Constitution of the United States, then who can I tell?"

"Well now," Hamilton said, taking off his hat and waving it in front of his face, "isn't that a hell of a thing."

"We thought that either you or Burr might know something," Swift said. "That is, after we'd figured out about this parallel time business." He didn't mention how recent that was. "Do you think Burr—"

"No," Hamilton said, "I don't."

"You think he feels strongly enough about it not to desecrate—"

"Not that," Hamilton said. "The other way around. You must realize that to those of us who drew up the Constitution, there is nothing sacred about the document itself; it's merely the working copy. What we regard as sacred, if anything, would be the thoughts, ideas, compromises, and dreams that we put into drawing it up. And those can not be stolen as long as the words are known."

"You're saying that to you the document itself was just a piece of paper," Swift said. "Then who . . . ?"

"Obviously, someone for whom the symbol is more important than the idea," Hamilton said. "Someone from Prime Time, perhaps; they're the sort of crass, thoughtless nitwits who would do this sort of thing."

"What is this 'prime time' business?" Swift asked.

"How can you not know that and still be following me around?" Hamilton demanded. "Never mind, we'll get to it later. Right now, we must debark and catch our train."

The boat pulled up to the Xantitipetal dock, the oars were shipped, the lines were thrown, and the gangplank dropped. Hamilton and Nate Swift were the first passengers off, and they rushed to a taxi-stand row of palanquins at the foot of the pier. They boarded the lead palanquin, and the four bearers dog-trotted them a couple of miles to a large, open-air railroad station.

"I thought these people hadn't even invented the wheel," Swift said, staring at the great, gadgety-looking locomotive and the overly ornate, but flimsy-looking passenger cars.

"Their gods have done a lot for them recently," Hamilton said. "Not only the wheel, but the steam engine, springs, iron, movable type, paper, and the grape."

"And in return they provide the labor to make everything work, right?" Swift said.

Hamilton nodded. "Simplicity itself."

They climbed aboard one of the carriages, which seemed to have been reserved for Hamilton, and settled on the wicker seats. One of the palanquin bearers clambered up onto the roof and disappeared from view. "My man," Hamilton explained, with a wave of his hand.

"What service does he provide on the roof?" Swift asked.

"He stays on watch for savages. He also runs errands."

"It must be hard to run anything across the roofs of these coaches," Swift observed. Hamilton shrugged, disinterested.

Two men opened the door to the carriage and deposited a large wicker basket on the floor. "Ah!" Hamilton said, rubbing his hands together. *"Goobish parmisan,"* he said to the two men, who bowed to him and retreated backward through the door. "Food," he said to Nate Swift. "Want a bite?"

It had, Swift realized, been a while since he'd eaten. A long while. "Yes," he said. "Thank you."

"Wouldn't want you to complain about the hospitality," Hamilton said. "We're going to be sharing this portable room for quite a while."

"Oh?" Swift said. "Where are we going? How long will it take?"

"Manhattan," Hamilton told him. "It should take about a week, barring wandering herds of buffalo blocking the track, or wandering savages burning the train."

"Sounds great," Swift said. "Why?"

"Because that's where my business is," Hamilton explained patiently.

"I mean," Swift corrected, "why such a laborious and time-consuming method of travel?"

"What would you suggest?" Hamilton inquired. "The aeroplane is a bit beyond their level of civilization. You have no idea how much work it was to give them the ideas for iron rails and steam boilers. Benjamin Franklin was a great help in that. You should meet him in Manhattan. I assume he is one of your childhood heroes also; he certainly deserves to be. Why that man has invented *everything.*"

"He is," Swift said. "But what I meant was: what about the gadget that brought us here, the transporter; why can't we just travel by that?"

"We can only go where It goes," Hamilton said. "Don't you know *anything* about the Prime Time, the It and all of that?"

"I guess I'm just culturally illiterate," Swift said.

"Well, it's very foolish to use a device without having a clear idea of what it is and how it works," Hamilton said. He opened the top of the wicker basket and delved into its contents, pulling forth a stoneware jug of wine and a baked-clay chicken. "Pull that flap at the side of the window," he instructed "That leather thing. That's right."

Swift pulled, and a folding table descended and unfolded itself between them. Hamilton put the comestibles on the table, and produced two stemmed glasses, two china plates, and two sets of silver. "Hm," he said. He dove back into the basket, and came out with two linen napkins. "Crack open the bird," he said.

Swift picked up the clay chicken and examined it. Hamilton handed him a small wooden mallet. "Carefully," he said. "Don't get clay all over everything."

Swift put the bird on the table and gingerly tapped at it with the mallet. The clay cracked, shedding powder, slivers and chunks, then it neatly fell into two halves, and a baked chicken emerged.

"Well done, sir," Hamilton said. "You may dissect it." And he handed Swift a small, triangular-bladed knife, quite sharp in edge and point. "I'll have a leg, to start with."

While Swift carved the chicken, Hamilton opened the jug, sniffed suspiciously at the wine, poured himself a taste, sampled, nodded approval, and poured out two glassfuls. Then he reached back into the hamper, to pull out a folded-up paper bag with a large red S, and the motto *Since we're neighbors, let's be friends* on the side. Opening it, he brushed the clay fragments into it, refolded and stuck it back in the hamper. "Neatness above all," he said. "Civilized man must always strive for neatness; it's the first thing to go."

Swift handed him a baked chicken leg, which he began to munch on reflectively. There was a series of sudden jerks, and the Intercontinental Coach began its Eastern Trek.

FOURTEEN

||||||||||||||||||||||||||||

The cell they stuck Ves in was one they reserved for friendly prisoners, since he had agreed to talk. After spending a couple of hours in it, Ves was becoming increasingly glad that he was not classified as an *un*friendly prisoner. If this was what they did for people they liked . . . four feet square it was, and five-and-a-half feet high. A two-by-four foot mattress of straw ticking took up half the floor, and sopped up the moisture which seeped through the floor and dripped from the walls. The only light came through the six-inch square hole in the door, which had three half-inch thick bars down and three across. "What the hell do you need the bars for?" he asked the guard who threw him into the cell. "No one can crawl through a six-inch square."

"Shut up," the guard explained, slamming the door with more than necessary enthusiasm and catching his thumb in the bolt. Muttering threats, and words Ves was glad he couldn't understand, he stalked away.

Some hours later, two men brought him a pewter bowl of dinner. It was milky-colored and rancid-tasting, but there wasn't much of it. A mug of well-aged water, perhaps a bit past its prime, but with a delicate bouquet, completed the repast. Then they came and took the utensils and pottery back. Then they left him alone.

After an unknowable length of time alone; a time certainly greater than an hour and less than a week, a time after his first meal and before his second, the girl came to him. She was small, slender and dressed in satin; a red jacket trimmed with fur, red riding pants, and high, black boots; her hair was long and red (chestnut? brown? it was so hard to tell in the half-light). Her features were patrician, and her voice was soft and foreign and carried the inflections of the Orient. "Good mahr-nink," she said, and it was like the trill of birds and the ripple of a slight waterfall.

The guard let her into the cell, locked the door behind her and went away.

"Good morning," Ves said, sitting up on his damp mattress ticking. "It is morning? Welcome to my humble abode. I've heard of progressive penology, but this is the first example of it I approve of. How long do you stay? Do you do windows, or just light housework? Can you cook? My terms are generous: I offer Sundays off, every other Thursday, and a half-day Saturdays. I like my three-minute eggs done for no more than five and a half minutes; and my toast burnt on the top only, no use turning it over, because I can tell, you know; jam yesterday and jam tomorrow, but never jam today. Am I babbling? You're the first person I've had to talk to in weeks. Just this dumb guard who yells 'shut up' and hits his thumb on things; very unimaginative. Weeks."

"You've been in here since late this (she said 'dees') afternoon. It now about ten o'clock in the evening (she said 'eef-nink'). But if it pleases you to bubble, go right ahead."

"Who are you?" Ves asked. "If they didn't send you as my live-in maid, what are you doing here?"

"*Tovarich*," she said. "I glad you asked me that."

"What was that first word," Ves asked. "I'm afraid I didn't quite catch it."

"You don't have to be afraid," she said. "I your *droog*. I not one of them. I not the Russian you think."

"I'm prepared to think you're any sort of Russian you like," Ves said, edging away from her. "How did you get in here?"

"Imperial Russia has friends among the guards; and I

have friends among the officers," she said. "You are to come with me."

"Who sent you," Ves demanded, "and where are you taking me?"

"Your *droog* Captain Richardson sent me," she said, "and I am to take you to the nearest Eet. Unfortunately, it is some distance away."

"Oh," Ves said. "Then you're not a Russian; you're Prime, like Richardson. You're from the Directory?"

"You bubble again," she informed him. "Of course I am Russian. I am not from this Time, but I am certainly Russian. In my time it is Nineteen forty-seven, Gregorian."

"Ah!" Ves said. "You're a Stalinist."

"A which?" she asked. "I am Countess Tatiana Petrovna Obrian: I hold the rank of Colonel in Secret Service of Tsar Alexander the Seventh."

"A countess in the secret service?" Ves asked. "Isn't that a bit unusual?"

"Certainly not," she snapped, drawing herself up to her full five-foot four, her eyes blazing. "Would you ask a peasant to spy?"

"I guess not," Ves admitted. "It's a pleasure to meet you, Tatiana Petrovna; I am Amerigo Vespucci Romero, prisoner of his Democratic Majesty, Jacob Schuyler."

She clicked the heels of her boots together and bowed from the waist. "A pleasure," she said. "We might be political antagonists in home worlds, but as fellow travelers sideways through time, we must aid each other, depend on each other, love each other. Russians good at love." She looked at him suggestively, relaxing her rigid military pose.

Ves shook his head. "You go too fast for me," he said. "One second you're clicking your heels, and the next you're talking about love."

"It is the complex Russian character," she told him. "It is why we are so sad." She removed an iron key from her boot and inserted it into the keyhole. "Contrived," she said. "They want you to escape, they give you key. No prisoner ever wonders why is keyhole *inside* of door. Most cells, is not keyhole inside door. Come, we leave now."

"Your accent seems to be thickening," Ves commented, following her into the hall.

"I am feeling patriotic," she told him. "Keep voice down." She tiptoed down the corridor to the far end, where an iron door on massive hinges barred their way. "We get out by going in," she whispered to Ves. "This leads to inner courtyard, now closed off and used as exercise yard for those prisoners who are allowed and able to exercise." Another key opened this door, and locked it behind them. "This way," she said, "to right. Leads to courtyard. Straight ahead leads to recalcitrant prisoners' block. *Ochen* disgusting. Come."

She led; Ves followed. Down the narrow corridor they hurried, to a thick, barred, wooden door at the end. There the countess paused, with Ves behind her, and there they waited.

"What's the matter?" Ves asked, in an urgent whisper.

"Nada," the countess said. "Nothing. I have not the key for this door, so we must wait until it is opened from the other side."

"By anyone special?" Ves asked, "or are we waiting until someone just happens by with the key?"

"I have a confederate in the courtyard," Tatiana Petrovna whispered harshly to him. "He will open the door."

"When?" Ves asked. "What is he waiting for? I mean, they're liable to notice that I'm gone any time now; they just might come looking for me out of spite."

"Pah!" the countess said. "No chance. They suffer from inefficiency and conceit, and the combination is fatal. If anyone comes for you and you are not in your cell, he will assume that someone else has already removed you for some official purpose: delousing perhaps. He knows you cannot escape, you see; because no one ever escapes. When anyone ever does escape, they are ashamed to mention it and write down that the prisoner either died or was released."

"The guard won't notice that I'm gone?" Ves asked.

"Pah! The guard. Pah!" The countess dismissed this menial with a wave of her hand. Just at that moment a gong started ringing in a far section of the building, and the sound of running feet could be heard down the corridor.

"What do you suppose that is?" Ves asked, pressing up against the wall and trying to melt into the stone.

"The guard has discovered that you have escaped," Tatiana Petrovna explained.

"Do you think we could convince your friend on the

far side to open this door?" Ves asked. "I don't want to seem anxious—"

"He will open it at any second now," the countess said. "The door is quite thick, and we can't yell for him; so he is opening it at a prearranged time."

"Which is how far off?" Ves inquired.

"I do not know," the countess said. "I have no watch."

Before Ves had a chance to think about that, the door creaked, shuddered, groaned, vibrated, and swung open. A tall man in a Hussar's uniform, complete with saber and busby, embraced Tatiana Petrovna, pulled them both through the door, and closed it. "Come along," his voice boomed in the courtyard, "I am tired of crouching innocuous in the corner. Let us get away from here."

"Lead the way," Ves said.

"No," the tall man said. "The countess leads; I stay last, to influence those who would follow." He touched his sword, and nodded significantly.

"You've convinced me," Ves said. "Let's go!"

"Keep against the wall," Tatiana Petrovna said, "someone may be looking out from an upper window."

The courtyard was a long, narrow area, walled by five stories of brick building on all sides, and floored in cement. The ground floor windows were sealed closed by iron shutters, the second and third floor windows were heavily barred, the fourth floor windows were encased in thick iron mesh, and the fifth floor windows were open. "I suppose those are the executive suites," Ves muttered.

Tatiana Petrovna inched forward, her back pressed against the wall; then she stopped and shook her head. "Is stupid!" she announced. "Sneak like criminals and anyone who sees you knows you are criminal. Proceed in self-assured manner, and he thinks you are guard—or maybe warden. We will proceed in self-assured manner!" She strode into the direct gloom of the central courtyard, then turned around and beckoned to the men. "Come!" she said. "Stride like a Cossack."

At the far end of the courtyard was a short flight of cement stairs, going down, leading to a painted metal double-door. They strode like Cossacks to the doors, and paused while the countess opened them. "Storeroom behind kitchen," she whispered. "We now pass through kitchen and to side exit door. Simple—no problems."

They entered the storeroom, closed and sealed the

door behind them. It was a large, high-ceilinged room, lit by a pair of gas fixtures high on the wall at each end. It was stocked with cartons, kegs, cannisters, barrels, boxes, bins, and the sort of loose unaccountable effluvia that piles up in a storeroom as the decades pass. There was a stack of rusted metal trays in one corner, a collection of cups of various patterns missing their handles on a shelf, and a broken machine that once stirred large amounts of something-or-other squatting by the door. They passed through the storeroom as rapidly and quietly as possible, and gathered at the inner door.

"Kitchen," Tatiana Petrovna whispered. "Might be empty; might be one-two cooks inside." She shrugged. "Pay them no attention and they will do the same. Head for side door to left. Ready?" Without waiting for an answer, she opened the door.

The light dazzled, and the sound clamored. The kitchen was a large expanse of spotless white, relieved here and there by a scrubbed wood counter top or a polished brass pipe. Scattered among the counter tops, ranges and sinks were groups of people in white smocks and white aprons, with floppy white hats or round white caps; tasting, stirring, seasoning and discussing. All such activity ceased when the door opened, all mouths closed except for those which opened wider in astonishment. All eyes stared at the three who emerged. A man in a deep red suit, fashionably tailored (at least Ves still wore his own clothing, and not prison stripes), a lady in a fur-trimmed jacket and pants (pants!) tucked into riding boots, and a uniformed soldier from no army that *they*'d ever seen.

Ves took one quick look at the situation and, smoothly closing the door behind him, turned to his companions and waved his right hand toward the gaping cooks. "This is the kitchen," he said loudly. "If Madam Commissioner will come this way . . ." He walked forward with an air of obsequious nonchalance. "Notice how clean everything is kept in the actual food handling area. Quite unlike the storeroom."

"Um," Tatiana Petrovna said, striding over to the nearest counter: "Um." She produced a pair of white gloves from an inner pocket of her jacket, ceremoniously put them on, then drew her fingers across the counter top and around the rim under the counter. "Grime," she said, examining the gloved finger.

"Grime?" Ves said, sounding incredulous. He turned to face the white-smocked horde and allowed his voice to rise. "Grime? *Grime?*"

Suddenly all the starers remembered something they had to do urgently, right now. They turned aside and stirred, checked the flame, washed the spoon, bowed the head, bent the knee, and averted the eye.

Tatiana Petrovna stalked haughtily through the kitchen without another word; behind her came Ves, wheedling and supplicating, "But Madam, they weren't prepared—but Madam Commissioner, you must give them another chance—I assure you they make every effort—this is normally the cleanest of kitchens . . ." . . . and so they passed through the door and out.

"Brilliant," the countess said, saluting Ves. "My carriage is on the next block. Let us go."

"Where," Ves asked, "are you taking me?"

"To the It," Tatiana Petrovna said. "We take you to Prime Time."

FIFTEEN

||||||||||||||||||||||||||||||

The train travelled twenty-four hours a day, pausing only to satisfy the engine's insatiable desire for fuel and water. Even so, the trip took almost a week: six days and most of the seventh. River fording, on great cable-pulled barges, ate up much of the time. Crossing the Mississippi took three trips and nine hours. The fuel was cordwood or soft coal; the only difference to the engine seemed to be in the color and intensity of the smoke it put out. During the stops food and water for the passengers was also hoisted aboard, but it was clear that no waiting would be tolerated for that. The train changed crews every day; one crew being on duty for twenty-four hours before being relieved at the appropriate water stop. Toilet necessities were provided for with the aid of specially designed carriage-pots kept under the seat. The design, Swift found, was poor.

Hamilton spent the time reading, expounding his theories of government, philosophy, religion, ethics, and morality to Swift, and writing in a thick daybook which he kept in his travelling-case. He seemed glad of Swift's company, and willing to answer any questions Swift had about what was happening, to the best of his ability. On the third day out, Swift asked him how he and Burr had gotten involved in the parallel time worlds.

"It was the duel," Hamilton explained. "You know about the duel?"

"Yes," Swift said. "On my world you, ah, got killed."

Hamilton nodded. "That conclusion seems predominant on worlds where the duel happened."

"It wasn't, ah, universal?"

"In some worlds Burr shot me and I lived; in most I died. In all we both fired, but I missed. At least, all I have any knowledge of. Which is very strange because I had no intention of firing; that is, I was going to discharge my piece into the air. But I aimed and fired. At least—" he shook his head "—*I* aimed and fired. I can only assume my doppelgangers did the same.

"In some worlds, of course, the duel didn't happen at all: either Burr didn't challenge me, or I contrived an honorable way to apologize for the insults in question. It is true: sometimes I let my mouth—or my pen—run ahead of my brain. I should never have said those things about Burr."

"What did you say?" Swift asked.

"I gave my opinion of Burr. I said he was a dangerous man and not to be trusted with the reins of government. I said more . . ."

"You didn't mean it?" Swift asked.

"Of *course* I meant it," Hamilton said, sounding annoyed. "Where I made my mistake was in saying it in public. Public, in this case, was a gentleman named Charles Cooper. Doctor Charles Cooper. He wrote a letter quoting me—half-quoting me, which is worse—which was published in the Albany *Register*. The letter said that I had uttered my 'despicable opinion' of Burr. You see, sir, in our society words are taken literally. What I had uttered was a *political* opinion of Burr. But despicable means personally vile, not merely politically contemptible.

"This was Cooper's word, not mine; but I was put in the position of having to defend it. If, when Burr called upon me I had retracted, my word would have been valueless, dishonored. And of course he had to call upon me: 'despicable' was not an epithet that he could, with honor, let pass. So we were forced by the code of our times to fight a duel that I'm sure neither of us really wanted."

"What happened?" Swift asked. "I mean, to you. Obviously, you weren't killed."

The train jerked and squealed to a stop; the high-pitched, agonizing sound of softwood brakes pressing against iron wheels. Hamilton and Swift were bounced forward and then back again, as the train came to rest. The sound of yelling carried clearly from the front of the train.

"There seems to be some earnest discussion going on up front," Hamilton said, opening his travelling bag and removing a pepperbox revolver. "We'd best go see."

They swung down off the carriage, Hamilton and his pepperbox in the lead, and trotted up toward the disturbance. The countryside was hilly and, except for the corridor cut for the train, heavily wooded. Because of the trees and a slight curve, the front of the train was just out of sight. The discussion seemed to be getting louder and more vigorous. A peculiar sound, half squeal, half bellow, was heard periodically. "Gods are fearless," Hamilton said, mostly to himself, and rounded the curve.

Hamilton stopped short. Swift caught up with him and also stopped. They stared, silently; there was nothing to say.

A line of camels stood in front of the train. Each camel wore a halter and a pack saddle. A group of gentlemen in long flowing robes and long, straight rifles stood beside the camels. Here in the forests of primordial Ohio, or Pennsylvania, a caravan was in front of their train.

Hamilton stood stock still for a minute, just watching the scene. "What's happening?" Swift demanded. "What are *they* doing there?"

"Only one way to find out," Hamilton said, and strode forward. "What's going on here?" he bellowed, trying to make himself heard over the Native uproar. "All right, let's have a cessation of yelling. What are you people doing here?"

One of the Arabs, a short, stout fellow, raced over

to Hamilton and grabbed his hand. "My dear man," he said, pumping it up and down, "You speak English. How delightful! Bentham at your service, Jeremy Bentham. Although, actually I'm afraid I'm the one who requires assistance. Would you be good enough to tell me where we are, and where the Great Desert is?"

"Desert?" Hamilton said. "There isn't a desert within two thousand miles of here. There's a nice desert a bit over two thousand miles West. West-south-west, to be more precise."

Bentham shook his head. "I've been misinformed. There's such a thing as being overly casual in giving directions. You're *sure* about that, now?"

"Sure," Hamilton said. He turned to Swift. "Mr. Swift, how say you?"

Swift nodded his head. "No desert around here," he said.

"Shocking," Bentham said. "Simply shocking. Never trust a Prime. Never again. What am I to do now?"

"As I see it, sir, you have two choices," Hamilton said. "Either follow this railroad line West until you cross a great mountain range, then turn left; or follow the line East some two hundred miles until you come to Manhattan, and use the It to return to Prime Time, whence I assume you came. If you are willing to abandon your camels, you can ride along with us and be there in a day. In either case, I must ask you to get your camels off our right-of-way."

"Of course, dear boy, of course. But what am I to do?" He put his hand under his chin and struck a pose. "I can't just leave the poor beasts . . . I'll follow behind you, old man. If we don't show up in a couple of days, send the dogs out to look for the camels, ha, ha, ha, ha." His chuckle had a dry and mechanical sound.

Bentham pulled his camels off the roadway, the Toltecs and their small god reboarded the train, and the journey resumed.

Hamilton produced a thin bottle and two small silver shot glasses from his baggage. "I think, perhaps, a small libation?" He poured. He extended one of the glasses to Swift. "Rum," he explained. "I always carry a small personal supply. There are so many places where you can't get it. Here, for example, they don't make it—yet. In many, ah, times, they don't believe in it. There was even times where they don't allow fermented beverages to be made: wine, or small beer, would you believe it?"

"I would," Swift said, taking the glass. He lifted it: "Your health, sir."

Hamilton nodded and raised his own shot glass. "And yours, sir; your very good health, indeed. You have proven a fine companion and excellent conversationalist on this long voyage."

Swift smiled. "You mean I listen well."

"I do indeed, sir," Hamilton acknowledged, with a smile of his own. "And a rare thing that is. I own that a great bit of any success I have had in life is due to my ears; I listen well and carefully. Washington valued me for my habit of listening to him. Everyone else either stared at him respectfully, too awed to hear what he was saying, or stared absently past him, too busy framing their rebuttal to care what he had said. *I* listened. I didn't always agree, but I listened."

"You were telling me about the duel," Swift reminded him.

"Ah, yes. The duel. It changed my life. Which is, I suppose, all to the good: in other time-lines, it killed me.

"In order to properly understand what happened and why, you must know that Burr and I are a nexus-point in history. By this I mean, if you trace historic lines in adjacent time-tracks to discover where they converge—or diverge, depending on which way you're going—you will find that they come together in bunches, all at the same point, like the straw in a broom. Actually 'point' is too confining a word: it's more of a, a blob." Hamilton clenched his left hand into a fist and held it out for examination. "A finite period of time covering one event, or one group of people.

"Well, Burr and I seem to be the focii of one of those times covering a period of about ten years starting in 1802 or so. There are whole sets of time-tracks where Burr was President, where I was, where he was Emperor of Mexico, and where the duel was fought with varying results. The histories of thousands of Americas in thousands of parallel time-worlds are dependent upon what Burr or I did, or didn't do, from 1803 till about 1812."

"Fascinating," Swift said, seeing that Hamilton had

paused for his reaction. "It must give you a strange sense of power."

Hamilton stared sadly into his silver glass. "It gives me a strange sense of fate, of destiny," he said. "I feel like some sort of marionette in a puppet play; and the puppeteeer keeps rewriting the ending."

"How did you get out of this cycle?" Swift asked.

Hamilton looked at him strangly for a second, as though he did not understand the question, then he nodded. "The duel!" he said. "That happened about five years ago now, my time, subjective time. Some Prime-Timers came to watch, you see, because it was such a famous, important event. They hid in the trees."

"So?" Swift asked.

"So, they are very careless, the Primes; thoughtless of what they do." Hamilton broke off and stared out the window. "This was the segment, you know, where Burr shoots me and I die in agony some days later," he said finally. "Like your segment, except I live a day or two longer and scream more. Everyplace I go, if it's uptime from my own time, I find out what happened to Alexander Hamilton. It's very sobering.

"Well, in this particular case, in this particular time, one of the Primes took a picture of the duel. A flash picture. It startled Burr so that his shot went wild, hit a stone, and ricocheted into the leg of the photographer. We were startled, he was displeased; it wasn't supposed to work out this way. I was supposed to be shot, and I wasn't. He was supposed to have a picture of me getting shot, and instead he had a ball in the photographer's leg."

"Don't these Primes have any sense of ethics in dealing with, ah, others?" Swift asked.

"Why should they have any more regard for those on the lower lines—that's what they call them, the lower lines—than we had for the Indians, or the Christians had for the Moslems, or the Catholics had for the Huguenots?"

"What happened?" Swift asked, refusing to get drawn into philosophy when what he wanted was facts.

"To me? I didn't die. To the Prime? We took him to a doctor. There was a surgeon waiting in the barge, but the Prime would have none of our primitive doctoring: he insisted on one of his own. He was perfectly willing to let *me* spend three days in agony dying, as long as he got his picture; but the thought didn't appeal as much when it was he who was doing the screaming. And at that, it was only a flesh wound. So we took him to one of his doctors—through an It. And our lives have never been the same."

"The experience of travelling through multiple worlds must be enough to entice anyone," Swift said.

"That's not it," Hamilton said, shaking his head. "It's the Primes. Not content with having ruined our duel; not content, I say, with saving life, they had to interfere further. There is some sort of rudimentary law in Prime Time about not interfering with the affairs of the lower lines. Something like your prohibition: the law seems to be there only to encourage the violators. However, in this case, as Burr and I were important to the very fabric of space-time (I quote, I assure you, I quote), they would have to do something about it. The Prime authorities spent large sums of money on my world to convince the citizens that I was dead and Burr was the murderer. As with everything else, they overdid it. I could never go back, as myself, since I was dead. Burr could never go back—they would have lynched him. A consummation most devoutly to be wished, perhaps, but not by Burr. Lynch came from Virginia, you know: Washington, Jefferson and Lynch, three shapers of American destiny, all from Virginia. It giveth one to pause."

"So what did you do?" Swift asked.

"What you see," Hamilton said. "I found a world which had a North American Continent inhabited only by un-civilized tribes, and I started my own civilization. With a few dozen picked people from different times as a core, and amenities obtained through the It, we will found here a republic of which Plato would be proud."

"What about the Indians?" Swift asked.

"What about them?" Hamilton replied, puzzled.

Swift shrugged. "Different points of view, I suppose."

"More of that democratic idealism of yours?" Hamilton asked. "You worried about the welfare of the Indians? My dear sir, when we came to this continent—to this version of our continent—the Toltec civilization was busily sacrificing people to the gods, in a particularly bloody manner, at the rate of about one a week."

"You've stopped that?" Swift asked.

"Well, we've at least reduced it, although many of the traditionalist priests are muttering about it. I don't know what we're going to do if there's a bad harvest, at any time within the next five years."

"I'm not convinced," Swift said. "There are always rationalizations for destroying someone else's civilization: they don't behave in a manner *you* consider gentlemanly. I think they have as much right to their customs as you have to yours."

"You wouldn't think so quite as eagerly if it was your chest being bared to the obsidian knife," Hamilton said. "But I'll make you a sporting offer: join our little society here, and have an equal voice in the changes to be made. What do you say, sir?" Hamilton leaned back, arms akimbo, and stared speculatively at Nate Swift.

"It's a nice offer, Mr. Hamilton," Swift said, "and I'll certainly consider it. But my present job is to find and restore the Constitution of the United States to its rightful place under glass. I have the additional job of finding my partner, Ves Romero, before we get too thoroughly separated by the sands of time."

"Good enough," Hamilton said. "I couldn't respect a man who dishonored a commitment. Find your friend, find that scrap of paper and return home. When you find yourself bored with your own world, come back here and take me up on my offer."

"How much trouble will there be in finding my own world?" Swift asked.

"In one sense, none," Hamilton told him. "In another sense, you'll never be able to find your own world, not ever again."

"What?" Swift demanded.

"In one sense, none——" Hamilton repeated.

"It was the second half of that," Swift said. "And don't bother repeating it, just explain it."

"Well," Hamilton said, putting his hand in front of his face and looking thoughtful, "I'll see if I can.

"The Intertemporal Transporter, because of some design feature in the Universe that it cannot overcome, something about bundles of energy, makes jumps of so-many millions or milliards of parallel times. Because of the slowing down—or speeding up, if you're going the other way—of the time stream, these jumps come some years apart in what I may refer to as the common history. Nine and seven-tenths years, to be precise.

"But, because of this gradual change in rate of the

time stream, a nine and seven-tenths years jump does not take you back to exactly the world you left; but to one a few tracks to the, ah, right, or left. Normally, these are so close to identical that you never know the difference. A man you will never meet might have taken on a different, unimportant profession, for example; or a building you will never see might be painted a different shade of green."

"That's all?" Swift said. "It doesn't sound like much. Still, it would be a funny feeling to know that somewhere, something is different, and you'll never be able to tell where or what."

"There is a chance, of course, that a major nexus point will come into the time flow between you and your home, and that you will land just on the wrong side of it. The chance is vanishingly small, but it is there."

"Wait a minute," Swift said, "don't you have to go back to the world where the It is?"

"Of course," Hamilton explained. "But that world has fissioned and split into parallel worlds many times since the It was planted there, and the It remains in each of them."

"Let me think about that," Swift said.

"Have another glass of rum," Hamilton offered. "It will clear your head."

SIXTEEN

|||||||||||||||||||||||||||||||

The two-horse brougham raced up Broadway as fast as the late evening traffic would allow. The Countess, sitting next to Ves in the rear seat, held his arm and bounced up and down joyfully. "Magnificent!" she said. "The quick thinking. The droll wit. The marvelous *ambiance*. 'This is the kitchen.' Oh magnificent! It is an honor to rescue you."

Ves nodded; he was sort of proud of himself. Cleverness is too often in the realm of the "I should have said", and to have been able to call upon it when necessary left a sort of smug afterglow. "I had to learn to think quickly in my business," he said. "Before I retired, in the early days when it was mostly repo work, we had to be able to be inventive at short notice."

" 'Repo work?' " asked the Countess.

"Automobile reposession. For banks, you know."

"What do banks want with automobiles?" she asked.

"Never mind," Ves said, "it'd take too long. I'd just like to thank you, and your Cossack friend here, for your timely intervention in my affairs."

"Think of it as nothing," the Countess said. "For now, the job of importance is getting safely to the It and away from this unfriendly time."

"Nate!" Ves said.

"What?" the Countess inquired politely. "I am unfamiliar with that expression."

"Nate!" Ves repeated. "My friend Nate, who is here with me; we must find him. We can't leave without Nate."

"We can," the Countess told him. "We must. He has not been arrested; I would have heard from Captain Richardson. Tell me where to find him, and I will see that a message reaches your friend."

Ves thought about it for a minute, as the carriage plunged on up Broadway. "You're right," he told the Countess. "The Gouverneur Morris Hotel on 34th Street, right off Fifth Avenue. If he's not there, try the Library." With a sudden little shock of memory, Ves felt in his pocket and found the transmitter pin. "As a matter of fact," he said, bringing the button up to his mouth, concealed between his fingers, and squeezing it: "Nate! Can you hear me, Nate? Are you there?"

Nothing, not even the hiss of static, which was automatically suppressed by the receiver.

"Why are you speaking to your thumb?" Countess Tatiana Petrovna asked. "Is it some sort of rite in your religion?"

"It's not my thumb," Ves said patiently, showing the tiny pin to the Countess, "it's this."

Tatiana Petrovna took the pin and examined it with cross-eyed intensity. "So," she said. "This is a fetish I am unfamiliar with. You're not a Christian Realist, are you: one of those people who do not believe in their own material existence, so they keep sticking pins in themselves to prove that they're here?"

"Not at all," Ves said. "That is a miniature radio transmitter. Do you have radio on your world?"

"Ah, da! You mean the spark-gap wireless mechanisms, and Vashinitsky Code with its blips and bloops. You send blips and bloops with that button?" She rolled the pin contemplatively between her thumb and forefinger, then handed it back to Ves. "Great for spies," was her final comment.

Ves pinned the button back onto the inside of his jacket lapel. "That's been thought of," he said.

The brougham pulled up at a large, squat building constructed of old red bricks. The bricks may have been new when the building was constructed; if so, neither aged gracefully. The driver hopped off his high seat and opened the door for his passengers.

The Countess emerged and stepped onto the sidewalk. "Nate what?" she asked Ves as he climbed down.

"Swift," Ves said, "Nate Swift. Nathan Swift."

"Very American," the Countess said, scribbling on the back of an envelope and handing it to the driver. "Here, proceed to the Gouverneur Morris and find Mr. Nathan Swift. Bring him after us."

The driver saluted and departed, leaping back into his driver's seat and flogging the tired horses into a new spasm of excitement as they galloped off.

"Boris, you will wait here," she told her tall Cossack. "Guard our retreat, if necessary. Follow in four or five hours with our friend's friend, or word of him."

He nodded assent. "Take care," he said.

Tatiana Petrovna turned to Ves, "Come!"

"You're taking me to Prime Time now?" Ves asked, following her through the narrow door in the brick, and into a darkness as deep as the space between the galaxies.

"Yes," her voice came, "but the way is long and not always safe." Her hand reached out and took his. "Come, let me guide you; I know the way through the dark."

Ves allowed himself to be led along a twisting path through what must have been several rooms or corridors. Only once, for a short distance, could he touch a wall on either side. "You certainly do know your way," he told her, his voice coming back to him as a hollow echo.

"Once my feet have walked any path," she said, "I no longer need my eyes to repeat the walk. It is a useful skill in my peculiar profession. Keep your voice down." She turned once more to the left, twice more to the right, and then halted. "We are there," she said positively. "Have you a match?"

"I don't think so," Ves whispered. "They cleaned out my pockets when they were interrogating me."

"I too am matchless," the Countess said. "I do not smoke. At times I burn, but I do not smoke. No matter, I shall proceed by touch. I must let go of you, as I need both hands. Put your hand on my shoulder or around my waist, to insure our togetherness at the critical moment."

Ves put his hand around the slim, feminine waist that was as firm to his touch as spring steel. "I wouldn't want to jeopardize our togetherness at the critical moment," he said.

"We Russians have no sense of humor," Tatiana Petrovna told him. "Was that funny?"

Ves sighed. "Ten years ago, I would have thought it romantic," he said. "But now, I suppose, it's funny."

"That is maudlin," the Countess said. "Age is merely a state of mind. Do not say sad things to me because I may cry. Russians are good at crying; but I won't be good at anything else for hours if you make me cry. I put myself into it wholly."

"I thought that was funny too," Ves said. "I guess we Etruscans have no sense of humor either. But we make great potsherds. How's it coming?"

"The wall is open," she told him. "I am fondling the dial even now. Results any second. Be patient."

Ves waited patiently, wondering how the Countess could travel so precisely and manipulate things so accurately in the blackness. An instinct "we Russians" have acquired through the long winters, no doubt, he thought. It was a shame that the light from the window high on the wall to his left was so faint, or it might be useful, Ves thought. Then, with a start, he realized that the window hadn't been there a second ago.

"That should have done it," Tatiana Petrovna said.

"It did," Ves assured her. "We are now elsewhere. Else-when? Well, wherever it is, we're there."

"Very good," the Countess said. "That's step one. Now we must proceed to the site of step two."

"This isn't Prime Time?" Ves asked. "Why don't we just go straight to Prime Time?"

"It doesn't work like that," Tatiana Petrovna told him.

"It goes where it goes, and we must follow it as we may. Each individual It goes through a limited number of parallel times following a definite pattern. Think of it as having to transfer to a number of different trams to get to your destination."

"So this is a sort of bus stop," Ves said, trying to make sense of the shadows passing outside the high window.

"But the next, ah, bus doesn't come to us; we must go to it," the Countess said. "It is not far. Judging by the window light, it is either late evening, or early morning. I do hope it is early morning: there are less objectionable people about at this very objectionable bus stop."

"What's objectionable about it?" Ves asked, peering into the gloom. "Where are we? Is it still New York? How many more transfers are there before we get to Prime Time?"

"Patience, and stay close to me," Tatiana Petrovna said. "God knows what will happen if we get separated here. It is still New York, I believe; but you will find little similarity to any New York you are familiar with, except for the name. Come."

She led him through the blackness to a wide entrance hall, which was semi-lit by two dim, uncovered incandescent bulbs set high up on opposite sides of the hall. There were thick black drapes hung on the walls, covering what must have been windows, and a black curtain shielding the door.

As their feet tapped hollow echoes across the tiled floor, Ves suddenly realized that he was cold. By the time they reached the black-curtained door a few seconds later, he had modified this feeling to *damn* cold: overcoat cold; parka cold; crawl under the covers and forget about going out today cold; stick your hands under your arms, stamp up and down and contemplate building a fire on the living room rug out of broken pieces of dining room furniture cold. And his brand-new, gaudy red suit jacket wasn't even *lined*, for crissakes; and the waistcoat had a false back (all in fashion, the tailor had told him, better for the line of the garment). And they were still inside the building. Ves didn't think he wanted to go out.

"It's cold," he said, tucking his hands under his arms and stamping his feet.

"You think this is cold?" Tatiana Petrovna snorted. "Wait until we get outside. The wind whips down the streets like February in Siberia. But at least there the snow isn't half-melted into that disgusting slush. Wait! I seem to remember concealing a blanket in this room somewhere for use in such emergencies. I will find it for you." She prodded and poked a couple of stuffed chairs that sat mouldering in the corners, lifted the cushion from one of them, and discovered a neatly-folded blanket of some thick material and dark color, which she threw to Ves. It smelled of horse.

Ves eyed it speculatively, then decided that he disliked the cold more than the smell and wrapped it around his shoulders.

"You should wear it with more élan," the Countess said. "You look like a peasant."

Ves shrugged. "How can you wear a horse blanket with élan?" he asked.

"Wear it as a cape," the Countess told him. "Throw it about your shoulders with a casual air. In the dark, who can tell?"

"It's warmer this way," Ves said. "Where do we go from here?"

Tatiana Petrovna raised her right hand, palm up, in a gesture that could have been acquiescence. "Have the goodness to follow me," she said, and pushed her way through the curtain. The wooden door behind it sagged badly on its hinges, but it must have been well greased recently, for it opened soundlessly to the street.

It was, Ves noted without real enthusiasm, no colder on the outside than it had been inside; but it was a good deal wetter. Mounds of snow had formed by the buildings and the curb; but in the street and sidewalk there was a layer of slush. The cold of the preceding night had managed to freeze a crust of ice over the slush, which gave Ves something to break through with every step. His shoes, thin-soled, square-toed, hand-stitched, buckle-closed shoes, rapidly became one with the slush.

"Stay close to the buildings as much as you can," Tatiana Petrovna told Ves, as she led him down the street with the rising sun at their back.

"Why?" Ves asked, seeing nothing unusual about the middle of the street. There wasn't even any traiffic around, perhaps because of the earliness of the hour. An occasional car parked along the curb dated the era to late-thirties, early forties, as well as Ves could tell.

"Snipers," she said.

Ves stayed as close to the buildings as he could. "How far have we got to go?" he asked.

"A few miles," Tatiana Petrovna said. "Maybe three. Not too bad. Can you drive one of these things?"

Ves stared at the closest car, which looked very much the way an old car was supposed to look. It was a HENRY *Tourglide Inline*. Ford or Kaiser, Ves wondered. "I can drive it," he told the Countess. He tried the door, and found it unlocked. "Get in."

"Can you start it without a key?"

"Any private detective could," Ves said. "It used to be one of the requirements for your license, along with keeping a bottle of booze in your desk drawer and refusing to handle divorce work." He popped up the hood.

Ford, he decided, examining the engine compartment with a professional eye. In a few seconds the engine had coughed into life and was settling down to a noisy purr, and he had slammed the hood shut and climbed behind the wheel. "Pretty good for an old man," he said, running the floor shift lever through the gears a couple of times to get their feel. "Where to, Lady?"

"Please," Tatiana Petrovna told him, "I am a woman, I am a countess, but I am no lady. The English are ladies. And you are not knowledgeable despite your age, but rather because of it. I cannot understand the American reverence for youth. The only thing the young have in their favor is a certain nimbleness of body, which is seldom matched by an accompanying adroitness of brain. The Empire State Building."

"Don't lecture me, Lady," Ves said, "I'm old enough to be your father." He smiled and stretched, rubbing his back against the rough fabric of the back of the seat. "Here we go," he said, shifting into first.

"Slowly please," Tatiana Petrovna said, "and keep the lights out." She was huddled up against the far door, staring earnestly out of the side window.

"Snipers?" Ves asked.

The Countess shrugged. "Anything. There is a war on here."

"What war?" Ves asked.

"The Second World War," she said.

"But there was no fighting in New York during World War Two," Ves said.

"In your world there wasn't," she said. "In this world, the Germans invaded New Jersey by giant troop-carrying submarines. I think that's right. My knowledge of the time is sketchy."

Ves drove the sedan slowly down the street. "I find that hard to believe," he said. "I mean, I do believe you, but I find it hard to accept that it's true. One thinks of the past as immutable, even if you can travel through it. The shooting of your grandfather paradox, and like that."

Somewhere, off in the distance, a machine gun sounded its staccato cough as Ves finished speaking. The sharp cracking sounds of several rifles came in immediate reply.

"You must understand that this is *not* time travel in any sense of the word," Tatiana Petrovna said, calmly ignoring the distant sounds. "Your past—the past of your particular world—is dead and gone, irretrievable as far as I know. This world is not behind your world in time, but somewhere off to the left, or right of it. Watch out for that tank!"

Ves swerved just in time to miss a tank that came lumbering around the corner on their right. The tank's turret swiveled around, the cannon seeking them as they passed. Ves flipped the steering wheel over hard left, bounced the car up on the far sidewalk, and then turned sharply right again until he reached the corner, where he spun the car around to the left and was out of sight around the corner building before he drove the car back down off the curb.

"Good driving," the Countess said firmly. The glint of excitement showed in her eyes, but otherwise she was completely unruffled. "But why did you go to the left? The tank's gun was turning to the right, so you passed right under it to reach the curb."

"The tank came from the right," Ves said, "so I knew I wanted to turn left and avoid meeting any of his friends. I thought it would be a good idea to get over to the left side of the road as quickly as possible."

"Good thinking," the Countess approved.

"That was a Sherman tank," Ves said. "I studied old armor and ordnance for a while."

"So?" Tatiana Petrovna asked.

"So it's one of ours. I mean it's American."

"So? I understand they're good shots, the Americans."

"I know what you're saying," Ves said. "But it does feel funny to have to run away from your own people."

Tatiana Petrovna nodded. "It does," she said. "I also have had to do that."

Ves turned downtown on Amsterdam Avenue, proceeding slowly, cautiously, and with his lights out. The dawn was beginning to light up the city, and now Ves could get a better idea of what the buildings he was passing looked like. The area was mostly five- and six-story brownstones, with a few storefronts and a couple of older, twelve- to fifteen-story apartment buildings. Every window up to the third floor in each building was boarded up. The storefront windows were taped and sandbagged, except for the ones which weren't there. Many of the building fronts bore the pockmarks of rifle or machine gun fire; a few showed the larger craterings of aircraft cannon, and an occasional pile of rubble showed the effects of artillery or bombs. Major damage was rare, but most of the buildings showed signs that people were trying to kill other people.

Tatiana Petrovna's hand clutched Ves's shoulder. "Pull over and stop," she said. "Quickly!"

Ves pulled the car over to the curb and set the brake. Two blocks ahead a pair of halftrack troop carriers ground their way around the corner, blocking the road. Men in field gray uniforms and bucket helmets swarmed off the backs, lugging heavy machine guns, steel boxes of ammunition, and sandbags, to commence construction of a barricade. They worked with the sure, instinctive knowledge of ants building an anthill, and the barricade took form with impressive speed as Ves and the Countess watched.

"The automobile engine is still on," the Countess said. "If one of the soldiers comes this way, he will probably hear it and investigate."

"I can stall it out," Ves told her, "and I will if I have to. But I can only start it again by going under the hood, which would make me sort of conspicuous. Let's sit here for a few minutes and see what happens."

As they watched a third halftrack joined the other two, and the soldiers began to fan out and occupy the buildings flanking the corner. Selected windows on the upper floors were knocked out, presumably to give marksmen stationed there greater fields of fire. Then a truck came up and off-loaded a steel-and-cement jigsaw puzzle that the men began erecting from sidewalk to sidewalk across the facing street, in front of the machine guns.

"Instant tank trap," Ves said.

"I think we had better get away from here," Tatiana Petrovna said. "If the Germans do not shoot us, they will soon cement us in."

"You have something there, Countess," Ves admitted. "We need one sudden, definitive act to get out of here before they have an opportunity to get any of those guns trained on us." He stared reflectively at the street. "A U-turn, I think, and then a quick right at the end of the block—"

His planning was suddenly interrupted by a high-pitched mechanical scream, and the undercarriage of a propeller-driven fighter aircraft appeared in the sky over them. It made a shallow dive toward the Nazi-infested corner. A rhythmic roar of explosions blotted out all other sounds, and hundreds of thiry-caliber steel-jacketed bullets created a moving line of destruction down the middle of the street. The asphalt was chewed into little bits, leaving a residue of black, powdery smoke; a fire hydrant erupted, sending a plume of water five stories into the air; a car exploded with a belch and a sheet of red flame; and a score of German soldiers, frozen into a tableau position for the split-second of remaining life, scattered like leaves in the bullet-storm and lay broken in grotesque postures about the barricade. Then the plane was past, climbing beyond the roofs and into the tranquil sky from which it had come.

The half-track vehicles sat there stolidly, looking whole amidst the wreckage, but a small, fine pillar of black smoke rose from the center one. The one on the left was canted at a strange angle, as though it were a model placed carelessly on a miniature street. An officer in a high peaked hat had run from his protecting doorway and was emptying his handgun at the retreating aircraft. Aside from the sharp yap of his pistol and the roar of escaping water, the street was curiously quiet in the immediate aftermath of the strafing attack.

"There is an ancient Chinese curse about living in interesting times," Ves said. "I wonder how they would have felt about traveling through interesting times." He backed the car up and then executed a slow, precise U-turn. Nothing impeded him except dust.

"I hope the It in the Empire State Building is still accessible," Tatiana Petrovna said. "It will cause us much inconvenience if it is not."

"I just hope the Empire State Building is still there," Ves said. "If it's still standing, we'll find a way inside; you have my word."

Twenty minutes more of creeping, darting, and waiting in their stolen Henry, and they arrived at their objective.

"Well," Ves said, pulling over to the curb and stalling the car. "Where is the gadget?"

"Upstairs," the Countess told him. "Way upstairs, in the observation tower."

"I should have guessed," Ves said. "Let's hope the elevators are running." They left the car and raced across the deserted sidewalk to the Fifth Avenue entrance of the building. One of the doors was unlocked. They went in, cutting their pace to a fast walk, and went down the long arcade toward the elevator banks. "Is this the last It before we arrive at Prime Time?" Ves asked.

"One more," Tatiana Petrovna said. "But less of a problem to get to."

"Why isn't there one that just goes straight through?" Ves asked.

"The Translator can only go from one time to another when its base exists in both times," the Countess said. "Haven't you noticed?"

"Noticed what?" Ves asked.

"The similarity of the locations on both sides of the transfer," she said.

"Ah!" Ves said. "Yes, of course. Now that you point it out."

"State your business!" a young, earnest voice called. And then, as an afterthought: "Halt!" Ves and the Countess froze in place, and a young corporal with an ancient Springfield rifle stepped out of a doorway, pointing the weapon at them in an embarrassed manner. "Advance and be recognized," he said.

"Good going, Corporal, keep alert," Ves said. He took a couple of steps forward and lowered his voice to a conspiratorial whisper. "This is top-security work for the Manhattan project. Top Secret, classified with the British Most Secret. You'll want the password, of course. The civilian project Class-A Password for the day is Eider-down. What's your countersign?"

"Eiderdown?" the corporal asked, sounding unhappy. "That's not the code-word I was given." He shifted the rifle as though uncertain whether he should point the rifle at Ves, or hand it to him. He compromised on a sort of port arms.

"It's *not* the code-word?" Ves asked in amazement. "You *are* cleared for top-secret, aren't you?"

The boy shook his head. "I don't think so, Sir."

"You're *not*? Then what are you doing *here*?" Ves's amazement was complete.

Tatiana Petrovna touched Ves's arm. "We are, after all, under attack," she pointed out. "Things get mixed up—confused. It's not the corporal's fault, surely." She turned to the corporal. "What password were you given?"

"Central Park," the corporal said. "And the counter-sign is supposed to be Bronx Zoo."

"There," the Countess said, with an explanatory gesture to Ves. "Central Park! Surely you see ... "

"Of course," Ves agreed. "Listen, son: use your code-word for all of your people. You know—Army and all that. But if anyone else comes in with the password 'Eider-down', remember that your countersign is 'Pillow'. I'll see that the next change of guard has all five classes of passwords."

"Five?" the corporal asked. By now, his rifle was pointed at the mural of a woodnymph with a jackhammer on the corridor ceiling, and he was holding it loosely by the stock.

"Five," Ves reaffirmed. "It's a complicated war. Thank you, corporal. Stay on guard, there are some German troops about. Are the elevators working?"

"Yes, sir," the corporal said. "Far as I know. Operator's down in the basement; just ring for her."

"Very good, thank you." And they left the guard, and proceeded to the elevator banks. "I forgot all about eleva-tor operators," Ves said. "Where I come from, you do that yourself."

"A true democracy," Tatiana Petrovna said.

The elevator came for them after one ring and a great deal of patience. "Where to, gents?" the girl asked.

"All the way up," Ves said.

"Okay," the girl said cheerfully, closing the door behind

them and starting the elevator with that stomach-dropping surge so characteristic of the building. "But you'll have to change at the hundred and second; that's as high as I go."

When they got off at the 102nd floor, the tower elevator wasn't working, so they had to walk up the last three flights to the observation deck.

It was broad daylight when they emerged on the deck, eighty stories above the fog. Most of the land below them was shrouded in ground fog and low-lying clouds. To the east and south pillars of black smoke rose in several different places, but no details could be made out.

"Come," Tatiana said. She led Ves around the tower to a certain spot on the outer wall facing downtown, and pressed a concealed switch. The panel flopped open.

"A second," she said, groping in the panel for the right button. Then she closed the panel.

"Well?" Ves said.

"It's done," she replied.

"Where in the name of Minos did you come from?" a voice behind them demanded. They turned.

A man in a blue toga with gold trim, and a woman in a Grecian-style gown with her left breast bared were standing arm in arm, staring at Ves and the Countess. The man held a blue-steel automatic pistol pointed steadily at Ves's belt buckle. It wasn't cold anymore, Ves noticed.

Tatiana Petrovna took Ves's arm. "This is the wrong place," she murmured in his ear.

SEVENTEEN

||||||||||||||||||||||||||||

The Intercontinental Coach ran out of track on the Jersey side—or what would have been the Jersey side—of the Hudson. A flat-bed barge with a steam-driven paddle wheel took them from the Hoboken docks to the Battery at the foot of Manhattan. There were a clump of neat-looking brick houses around the Battery, an expanse of cleared land behind the houses, and then a dense forest covering all of uptown Manhattan. "So this is your colony," Swift said, stepping off onto the dock and gazing around at the neat, clean, geometrically precise brick walls. Even the dirt street seemed to have been scrubbed.

"Gentleman farmers," Hamilton said. "Jefferson would approve. Of course, *we* don't use slave labor."

"What then," Nate Swift asked doubtfully, "Indian workers toiling for their gods?"

"Don't be ridiculous, sir," Hamilton said scornfully. "Admittedly we used Indian labor to construct the great Intercontinental track; but the various tribes and nations involved considered that as an apparatus of the gods, and a device which would benefit them as they do use it for trade and commerce. But to ask them to grub around in the dirt growing maize for their gods would quickly disenchant them, I'm afraid. We should have to resort to ungodlike remedies to kep them with their hands to the plow."

"Don't tell me you do the work yourselves," Swift said.

"Have you never heard of indentured service, sir?" Hamilton asked. "It is a fair and honorable way of establishing yourself in a new country if you have no capital of your own." Hamilton led the way across the road to *Poor Richard's Tavern* as they spoke, and he ushered Swift through the stout oak door.

"That's a sort of slavery on the time-payment plan, isn't it?" Swift said.

"No," Hamilton said, and let it go at that while they sat down at the long wooden bench nearest the door and were brought two great pewter mugs of ale by a girl who could have been no older than fourteen. Then he turned to Swift and studied him closely, as though he were trying to memorize his face. "We've travelled together for over a week," he said, "and I confess I don't know you. You speak sense mostly, but you appear to have some strange Jacobin ideas. If a man has nothing, why should he not work to acquire something? Should it merely be handed to him? By whom? And from whom should it be taken away, and why?"

"I just don't believe that you can buy a man's life for a period of years," Swift said stubbornly.

"Not his life, sir," Hamilton said, slapping his hand down on the bench wood, "not his life. Merely his work. And they don't have to sell. We have no press gangs operating to supply us with forced labor. There are many people in many alternate Americas who would be delighted to have a chance to come here to Georgeland. Our recruiting is not a problem. On the contrary, we have a careful program to restrain growth and keep it in hand. We hope to learn from your mistakes."

"Georgeland?" Swift asked: "Georgeland?"

Hamilton shrugged, in what Swift had come to recognize as a characteristic gesture. "We could do no less," he said. "Although, I'm afraid, General Washington will never come to hear about it. The first rule for an invitation here is when there's serious trouble in your home time; and in every time where we've located General Washington still alive, he's doing quite well." He drained his ale and wiped his mouth on the lace cuff of his shirt. "Believe me, Mr. Swift, those who serve under indenture here are much better off than the millions who call themselves freemen in other places which are named the United States of America."

"I don't deny that," Swift said. "And I admit I'm favorably impressed both with your colony and your rhetoric. Very neat and clean, the both of them."

"Hem, sir," Hamilton said, "we shall not, at the moment, discuss politics of philosophy any further. Drink up your ale."

"We agree, sir," Swift said, taking a hearty swallow from his mug. The ale was thick and rich, and tasted strongly of the grain it was brewed from. It could have made a pleasing meal of itself, but Swift resisted the temptation to make it his lunch. "Any food available?" he asked Hamilton.

"It comes," Hamilton said. And sure enough a few minutes later it came: a giant platter filled with assorted cheeses, meats, breads, and pickled green things. And behind it came the landlord, a short, active man of middle years who looked very familiar to Swift.

"Alex," the landlord said, extending a large, calloused palm. "Welcome back. What news?"

"The recruiting goes well," Hamilton said. "The needed supplies are purchased or ordered. No news of Burr."

The landlord ritualistically wiped his hands on his apron. "Aaron Burr is your own particular bête noire, and none of the colony's affair," he told Hamilton. "Personally, I always liked the man."

Hamilton shrugged. "I'm not trying to incite you against Burr," he said, "but merely to keep track of him."

The landlord nodded and sat down opposite Hamilton and Swift. "True wisdom," he said, "consists of knowing your own motives. And what is this young man? I don't believe we've met."

Swift extended his hand. "Nathan Hale Swift," he said. "My pleasure."

"Named after one of us, I see," the landlord said, taking the proffered hand. "Like George Washington Carver. A fine tradition. My name is Benjamin Franklin. Unfortunately, not Benjamin Franklin anything, just Benjamin Franklin."

"Ah!" Swift said, shaking the calloused hand. He couldn't think of anything more to say that wouldn't sound silly, so he said nothing. The silence stretched toward the ridiculous.

"You have a curious reluctance to cease shaking hands," Franklin observed. "Is it, perhaps, your only form of exercise?"

"No, no," Swift said, jerking his hand back. "Sorry."

"I once invented a machine for shaking hands," Franklin said. "Thought it would be of inestimable use to politicians. None of them ever used it, though. Said it removed the personal touch. I told them that was its major value. Removing the personal touch of politicians is always a desirable goal in and of itself. Don't you agree, Alex?"

"I must leave now," Hamilton said, standing up, "and check on some matters of immediacy. I shall return. Please take care of Mr. Swift while I am gone. He has quite an interesting problem that he would love to share with you and seek your advice on. I have no doubt but that you'll give it." He smiled grimly, like a headmaster showing his students that he does have a sense of humor. "I leave you in each other's capable hands." And with that he strode out of the house.

"A problem, eh?" Franklin said, standing up and removing his apron. "A problem . . . or was Hamilton jesting?"

"No, sir," Swift said. "I have a problem. I don't know if you can help me, but I do have a problem."

"Excellent!" Franklin said. "Nothing keeps the brain stirred up and active like a good problem. Animal, vegetable, or mineral? Or perhaps spiritual? Here, let's go into my office and discuss it over a cigar. It's good Connecticut broadleaf."

"No, thank you," Swift said, as Franklin led the way through the rear of the common room to a spacious office, containing one of the finest, largest Colonial desks Swift had ever seen. "I don't smoke cigars."

"You don't, eh?" Franklin said, selecting one from his humidor and carefully cutting off the end with a golden cigar clipper. "Can't say as I blame you." He took a box of blue-tip kitchen matches from a drawer and used one to light the chosen cigar. "Vile habit. Vile. Dangerous, too, I understand. Would you like some bitterroot tea, or perhaps some sarsaparilla? What is your problem?"

Swift gazed intently across the desk. "I'm searching for the Constitution of the United States."

"An intellectual sort of pursuit, I'm sure," Franklin said, leaning back in his wooden chair with his hands folded across his ample middle and tilting his head sideways to stare at Swift through the upper half of his bifocals. "Does your search go to the original document, or are you searching in the writings of Voltaire, Plato, Lao Tzu, and Hamhotep the Scribe?"

"It isn't the ideas I'm searching for," Swift told him, "but the original document. In my world someone has stolen the Constitution itself: parchment, ink, and all."

Franklin's mouth fell open and his eyes crossed as he shifted his gaze to his thumbs, which were circling each other above his laced fingers. He remained in this posture of contemplation for a silent minute. Then he said, "Fascinating! The whole thing, eh?"

"Yes sir. Out of a sealed glass case with a helium atmosphere."

"Helium, eh. From the sun, you know. Helios is Greek for the sun. Gas, is it?" Franklin stood up. "Of course, in one sense it's nothing to get excited about. I mean, no one can steal the Constitution. It is in the hearts and minds of all Americans. Besides, it must be written in a million textbooks. But in another sense, it is a dastardly thing to do. Wonder how it was done. Case was unopened?"

"As far as anyone could tell," Swift said. "The internal helium atmosphere was undisturbed, at any rate."

Franklin stared off into space through the top half of his bifocals. "Can't do it, you know. Not as described. Some element is missing. The impossible is merely the

possible improperly described. Tell me about it in detail."
He sat back down and transferred his stare to his guest.

Swift told Franklin the story of the substitution in detail, chronologically; and Franklin listened silently, with
his eyes closed and his lips moving slowly in and out.
"Aha!" Franklin said at one point, "the essential detail!" But as Swift was talking about Burr's signature, and
it was unreasonable to assume that Burr had committed
the theft, Swift was not sure which was the detail.

"And so," Swift said, completing his tale, "I now not
only have to find the Constitution, but I have to locate my
companion, Ves Rómero. He is probably in trouble and
might be anywhere by now. Or anywhen."

"The two of you will, of necessity, come together
again," Franklin pronounced. "As you are both seeking
the same thing, you will both terminate at the same location. I use the word 'terminate' in its less final meaning."

"I hope," Swift said. "Besides, we're only going to
terminate at the same place if we have some way of figur-
ing out where that is."

"No problem," Franklin said. "I don't know who took
your, eh, particular Constitution, or why. But I believe I
can tell you how it was done, and where to look for it."

"You can?" Swift said, amazed. "From what I've told
you?"

"Simple deduction, my boy," Franklin said. "And if I
can do it so easily, surely someone from whom your companion seeks aid will be able to similarly guide him. Perhaps the necessary effort will be greater, but the result will
be the same." He pushed himself to his feet and maneu-
vered across the floor. "Would you like some spring
sausage?" he asked. "It's my own recipe: an adaptation of
one given me for *petite saucisse* in a small inn to the north
of Paris." He tugged a great bellpull by the side of the
door and, without waiting for a reply, yelled, "Maryanne,
child, bring some sausage and cheese on a platter, and
some ale in a pitcher. Bring them to the workroom." Then
he beckoned to Swift. "Come along," he said. "It's on the
other side of the house. There are some things I'd like to
show you."

"Certainly," Swift said, following along behind Franklin.
"But how *was* it done, and where should I look?"

"Patience," Franklin said. "He who is patient today
need not wait for, eh, dumpty um—something that rhymes

with 'day', however vaguely, would be nice. Need not wait for hair to gray . . . to find a lay . . . to stack the hay . . . I'd best let that one simmer a while longer, it clearly isn't done yet. At any rate, in a minute I'll show you how it was done. Probably done. Almost certainly done. Don't see how else they could have done it. And *that* should show you where to look."

Franklin's workroom was a large, detached room at the rear of the house, which bore the constructional signs of having once been a stable. In an incredible state of disarray, it bore family resemblance to a science-fair project, an alchemist's workshop, and a rummage sale. A giant Franklin stove dominated the center of the room; its stovepipe doing three right-angle turns as it climbed and finally disappeared through a hole in one corner of the roof. Three large worktables formed a tight triangle with the stove as their center. The tables were so full of a number of things that a fourth, temporary table had been set up by the door to work at.

"What on Earth is that?" Swift asked, pointing to a contraption on the righthand table that looked like a cross between an organ and a sewing machine.

"An invention of my own," Franklin said proudly. "It's a steam-driven typewriter. Changeable fonts. It'll come in very handy when I get it perfected. I am the publisher of the colony's only newspaper. A weekly. *Poor Richard's Thursday-Evening Post.*"

"Don't you need a typesetter, rather than a typewriter, for a newspaper?" Swift asked. "Not that I know much about journalism."

"Don't feel bashful," Franklin said. "Writing is the only field where everyone, practiced in the craft or not, feels that he's an expert by birthright. That goes for both the technical and the creative ends of the profession." He walked over to the contraption and prodded it a few times. "I'd give you a demonstration, but it takes half an hour to get the steam up.

"To answer your question, which I was not ignoring, I have developed a variant of the silk-screening process to produce my journal. The letters will be impressed directly onto a specially-treated screen, which will then be put in a frame, and ink rolled through the reverse when the frame is applied to the paper." Franklin used his hands to create what he was talking about as he described the process. Swift could almost see the press emerge out of the air as Franklin's rapidly-moving hands circumscribed it.

"Now to get to your problem," Franklin said. "Come look at this." He led the way across the room to the farthest table and waved his hand at a modest tangled ball of wires, tubes, coils, pipes, ceramic doodads, and carefully-carved ivory whatnots that occupied one end.

"Beautiful," Swift said appreciatively. "What does it do?"

"This apparatus is an Intertemporal Translator," Franklin said. "It moves objects from here to there; or perhaps from now to then. What can one say about a device which travels sideways through time?"

"You invented this?" Swift asked.

Franklin shook his head. "A great-grandson of mine manufactures them in a different time-line, but I don't even know how it works. I've got this one set up here to try and discover that very thing: how it works, what it is capable of doing; for that matter, what powers it. All mysteries. But we make some slow progress. Mostly in the sphere of what the device is capable of doing. What natural law it operates by and where it draws its power— if it uses power—are still unanswered questions, at least by this investigator."

The young girl who had served in the common room opened the door of the workroom and backed in, carrying a pewter tray of bread, sausage, cheese, and a pitcher of ale. She set these down on the near table, producing two mugs from under her arms and wiping them off with a towel before setting them down. Then she curtsyed and left. "Good girl, Maryanne," Franklin said, filling the two mugs. "Teaching her to read. There are those who don't hold with teaching a girl to read, but I ain't one of them."

Swift, who had been regretting the missed opportunity of eating in the common room, constructed himself a large sandwich and began to eat. "The Constitution," he reminded Franklin, "and the Intertemporal Translator."

"Yes," Franklin said. "Let me organize my thoughts." He closed his eyes, pursed his lips and his hands created universes in the thin air. Then his eyes opened. "I shall show you." He scrabbled about the table, picking up and discarding various small objects, before finally settling on a stone beetle about the size of a thumbnail. "Scarab," he said. "Sacred to the Egyptians. Given me by a Frenchman, who found it in a tomb. Says it's over three thousand years old. It'll do."

He fastened the scarab into the apparatus on the table. "This is an alternate use, you see," he said. "The way it's usually set up—the way this one was set up when I found it—it's built into something that's quite old, quite large, quite solid. It then somehow sends whoever uses it to the identical base object in another time line."

"Even if the base object is no longer in the same location?" Swift asked.

"Apparently," Franklin said. "As you should know, judging by your instantaneous trip across country when you translated with Hamilton. The important thing is that the two objects be identical; it doesn't seem to matter where they are. Now, what I have done is to alter the operation so that instead of sending *us* from object to object, it will change object for object, from another time to this. Here, watch." Franklin touched the switch on his apparatus. . . .

. . . and nothing happened. The scarab remained where it was, and changed not a scale.

"It didn't work," Swift said, trying not to sound as disappointed as he felt. For a second he could see possibilities that would have explained—

"Of course it worked," Franklin insisted. "How do you expect to be able to tell when two identical objects changed place?"

"Well, how do you know it happened?" Swift demanded.

"Easy to prove," Franklin said. "Wait a few minutes— the machine seems to have a short recycling time before it will work again."

Swift ate his sandwich and drank his beer and tried to moderate his impatience.

"Long enough," Franklin finally said, after what was certainly long enough. "Now watch!" He took a wooden mallet from a peg on the wall and brought it down squarely on the tiny scarab. The beetle shattered into sufficient fragments to destroy whatever identity it had held. There was nothing to show, now, that it ever had been aught but a pile of stones and a mound of dust.

"What does that prove?" Swift asked, shocked by the sudden destruction.

"Patience," Franklin said, setting the mallet back on its peg. He touched the switch again. . . .

. . . and the scarab was restored.

Swift stared at it. He picked it up and examined it closely. "It looks identical," he said.

"Better than that," Franklin said, "it *is* identical. It is the same, unique object. Somewhere in another time-line, in some tomb by the Nile, or in some Egyptologist's glass-topped case, is a small mound of fragments that were a few seconds ago a stone scarab."

"Hah!" Swift said.

"Do you see?"

"What?" asked Swift.

"That's how your Constitution was stolen," Franklin said triumphantly. "That's why an alternate copy, which tested genuine except for the, eh, discrepancy in autographs, was left. It must be the identical parchment on which your Constitution was inscribed. It just carried along that tiny bit of different ink when the switch was made."

"Hah!" Swift repeated. "It sounds good. Yes, I like it. I believe it. But then, why? Who would want to exchange our real Constitution for another real Constitution? It makes no more sense now than it did before I understood how it was done."

"That may be," Franklin said, "but at least it considerably shrinks your list of suspects. It almost had to be someone from Prime Time. No one else would have known how to use the It for such a purpose, or had a spare one at his disposal."

"You have one," Swift pointed out.

"Yes, that's true. But I am unique," Franklin said. "And I certainly didn't manipulate any copies of the Constitution of the United States."

Swift, deep in thought, finished his second sandwich. "I must go to Prime Time," he said, cleaning up the crumbs with the large square of linen provided.

"Of course, my boy," Franklin said, eyeing the remains of the food tray. "Would you like me to pack you a box lunch?"

"You mean it's that easy?" Swift asked.

"Of course, now that you're here," Franklin told him. "We have an It connection through to Prime Time, right here in Manhattan. Whenever you're ready to go, just speak."

"Well," Swift said. "I see. Um. Is there anything I

should know? I mean, is there anything you can tell me about Prime Time, or its citizens, that I would find helpful?"

"What sort of things?" Franklin asked.

"Well, for example: what about capital crimes? Do they put you to death for spitting in the street, or daring to look in the face of an unmarried woman? Is it against the law to go down Main Street without your roller skates on? Do the people regard an unbearded male as an offense against nature? Things like that."

"Sensible information to request," Franklin agreed. "Let's see what I can tell you.

"The people are so diverse, so unstructured, and so blasé, that almost any mode of dress or pattern of conduct that is not physically harmful will be inoffensive to them. Their major flaw, as far as I'm concerned, is that they really don't give a damn about anybody else. To the extent that it means that they're not nosy, and don't pry into your business, that's an excellent quality; but when it means they'll casually stroll by the spot where you're sinking in quicksand without sticking out a hand to help, I think it's a pernicious custom."

"But unharmful as long as I keep away from the quicksand," Swift said.

"I think it will eventually destroy their society," Franklin said. "But so long as the breakup doesn't occur while you're there, it should be harmless to you. That is true."

"I'll have to supress any philosophical objections until after I find the Constitution," Swift said.

"The man with the mission," Franklin said. "Very fine. I approve."

"I should like to sleep in a bed tonight, after a week on the berth in that coach. And tomorrow I shall go onward to Prime Time."

"My inn is yours while you're here," Franklin said. "Go off now and tell Maryanne to give you room six, and get some sleep. See me before you leave tomorrow; I might have some notions to talk over with you."

EIGHTEEN

||||||||||||||||||||||||||||

The toga'd gentleman looked puzzled, but the muzzle of his gun persisted in pointing toward Ves's midsection. "Where did you come from," he insisted, "and why are you dressed like that?"

"Make it good," Tatiana Petrovna whispered to Ves, with her body turned away from the Roman couple.

"We came from around the corner," Ves told the couple, indicating the curve of the observation tower off to the left. "Can't you get us out of here?" he whispered to the countess.

"Not for ten or fifteen minutes," she murmured, "then it has to recycle. Keep talking."

"Around the corner?" the man demanded. "Why are you dressed like that? Aren't you part of the tour?"

"The tour?" Ves asked. "Which tour is that?"

The man shook his head. "Evidently you're not," he deduced.

The bare-breasted young lady pulled at the Roman gentleman's arm. "Come on, Harry," she said. "We've got to get all the passengers checked in."

The man shook his head. "They might be dergs," he said. It sounded like "dergs."

"They're not dergs," the woman said. "Look at them. Come on now, we have to hurry—the dergs are probably halfway up the stairs."

"We never should have come," the man said. "I *told* them it was a poor idea. I don't know what to do." He looked at the woman, appealing for help.

"*I* don't know," she said. "And I really don't care what you do, but do something. We have to get the group boarded and out of here."

"Damn," the man said with feeling. "Look," he waved the pistol at Ves. "What are you two doing here?"

131

"We were trying to get away from the dergs," Ves said calmly. "There was nowhere else to go."

"Ah," the man said. "Then you're not dergs?"

"I assure you," the countess said, "we are not."

"Look at them," the Roman lady said. "Now let's get busy. They're not dergs. We have a ship to load."

"You're right," the man said. "You must have an interesting story," he told Ves. "We must talk later."

"Indeed we must," Ves agreed.

"Come on, Harry," the lady said. And she pulled him away, around the bend of the observation tower.

"Dergs?" Ves said.

The countess shrugged. "A totally different world; I've never been here before. Ship?"

"How does that happen?" Ves asked. "The totally different worlds, I mean."

"I can tell you *what* happens," the countess said. "But as to how—that can only be expressed mathematically, and I don't speak the language."

"Can we go yet?" Ves asked. "The dergs, whatever they are, are getting closer."

"Patience," the countess said. "If I push the button to soon it will drain off all the charge being accumulated, and we'll have to wait all over again."

"How did we get here?" Ves asked.

"It's the drift of the parallel worlds," Tatiana Petrovna said. "As new ones are formed by decision points, the old ones get further apart and their rate of progress through the time stream changes. Occasionally two get far enough apart so that one, which couldn't be reached before, appears between them when you use the Translator."

"I don't understand that at all," Ves said.

"Regardless, we are here," the countess said. "Relax and enjoy it."

"Let's hope our stay here is brief," Ves said, flopping onto the wooden bench along the inner wall. "I'd just as soon never find out what a derg is."

"The dergs," a high-pitched voice beside him said, "are black and have legs." Ves jerked around to find a solemn-faced small child in a toga staring at him. The child raced off, his sandals flapping on the tile.

"A great exit line!" Ves called after the child, as he disappeared around the bend.

"Another few minutes and we can try," the countess

said reassuringly. She sat down, unzipped her boots, and pulled them off, revealing a pair of bright red socks. "Must let my feet breathe for a minute," she said. "Take care of your feet and your feet will take care of you."

A woman with long blonde hair, wearing a classical Cretan dress, came running around the corner. "Have you seen a five-year-old boy come by here?" she asked.

"He went that way," Ves said, pointing.

"That boy could get lost in an empty set," the woman stated, heading off toward where Ves had pointed. A few moments later she came back through, with the boy in tow.

"I think we can try it just about now," the countess said, wiggling her feet one last time and pulling her boots back on. "You realize the calibration control is meaningless from this location, so I have no idea where we'll end up."

"Do you want to wait for the dergs?" Ves asked, shrugging his approval.

"I was just informing you." Tatiana Petrovna went back to the concealed niche in the wall and opened it.

"Here now," the Roman with the gun said, coming back around the corner, "what do you think you're doing?"

"Just getting a drink of water," Ves said at random. "Don't mind us. Go on with your tour."

"We can't have that, you know," the Roman said. "Close that now!"

Tatiana Petrovna hesitated for a moment, then swung the little hatch closed.

"That's right," the man said, "now come along with me. Time is getting short, you know. The dergs are due! Come along, now!" He waved them along with his automatic in a friendly manner.

"Great," Ves murmured to the countess. "A tour guide with a gun. Where the hell does he think he's taking us?"

A sudden burst of thunderous sound reverberated through the closed room. Ves swung around to see the Roman putting the automatic back in his belt. A great hole was now blasted in the concealed panel to the It. The panel swung open, and little bits and pieces of the device fell out onto the floor.

"Swell," Ves muttered. "I wonder what he thought he was doing."

"This may present a problem," the countess said, looking thoughtful.

The Roman trotted past them. "Come along," he said. "There's nothing here for us."

Ves and the countess followed him around the curve of the observation tower and there ahead of them—on the hundred and fifth floor of the Empire State Building—was the ship: a giant, silver, cigar-shaped dirigible, hundreds of meters long, swinging gondolas the size of ballrooms hung tight against the taut silver belly. The dirigible's nose was moored to the tower somewhere above them, and from a door in the observation room a flexible tube led to a corridor inside the body of the ship.

The man waited by the door. "Go on, go on," he urged. "You are the last."

Tatiana Petrovna shrugged. "Might as well, now," she said. They entered the tube, which was formed of ropes, with aluminum rods for flooring and fabric walls as thin as sausage skins. The aluminum framework corridor inside the dirigible, between the giant gas bags, seemed positively substantial by comparison.

After walking for longer than seemed reasonable, they came to the first ladderway down: straight down, with a sign beside it that said BRIDGE & OFFICERS' QRTRS RESTRICTED.

A bit beyond that was the next one, marked CREW ONLY. Then the third, which was marked FORWARD ENGINE ROOM—AUTHORIZED PERSONNEL ONLY.

About ten meters further came a spiral staircase, with velvet-covered handrails, labeled FIRST CLASS CABINS AND LOUNGES. "Are we first class?" Ves asked the countess.

"Are we not?" she demanded, and started down the stairs.

They went past two corridors of staterooms before coming to a lounge. The few people they met in the corridors, mostly dressed in Roman garb, treated them with total lack of interest. Given the circumstances, they could only be grateful.

The couches in the lounge were arranged so that you could stare out the portholes, which were angled down for a better view, while sitting comfortably next to your neighbor. Tatiana Petrovna and Amerigo Vespucci settled in a corner of the lounge and watched Manhattan Island recede beneath them. "What do we do now?" Ves asked.

"Humorous," the countess said. "I was about to ask you the same question. You realize what has happened?"

"What do you mean?" Ves asked.

The destruction of the It," she said.

"We'll just have to wait until we can get away from these people and find another one," Ves said. "Avoiding the dergs."

"I don't know if we can," she said. "Remember, I told you this world just became accessible to the It. In effect, as far as intertemporal travel is concerned, it just came into existence. There may not be any other Its here yet. It may have come into existence for the It we just used and for no other."

"Does that happen?" Ves asked.

"I think so. Remember, my group just rides on the coattails of the Primes; we don't know all the rules yet. But I've heard stories."

"Wonderful," Ves said. "I wonder how Nate is making out. Does that mean we're stranded here for good?"

"I wouldn't think so," the countess said. "As soon as the potential for coming here exists at the other Its, Primes or others will arrive here by accident, as we did. They will probably leave immediately, but the device will have been established. In another year or so we should be able to locate another It, if we persevere. Yes, I should say definitely within a year or two."

"Wonderful," Ves said. "If we don't get eaten by dergs."

"What *are* dergs?" the countess asked.

"I asked you first," Ves said. "What are dergs, and who are these people? What sort of an alternate track are we on?"

"Do you mean that philosophically, my friends," a rough, gravelly voice behind them inquired, "or is it an actual request for information?" They turned to look. A short man dressed all in black came down the aisle toward them. He had dark, piercing eyes under heavy brows, and a look of great intelligence and compassion. "Welcome aboard the *Titanic*," he continued, "I was told you were here."

"The *Titanic?*" Ves couldn't help asking.

"True," the man said. "Her name is wrote large across her prow. One of the Prime Exploration Fleet. Sister ship to the P.E.F.S. *Mary Celeste*, the *Morro Castle*, the *Kiche-maru*, the *Lusitania*, the *Normandie*, the *Andrea Doria*; is that ten?"

"No," Ves said. "Eight, I think—no, seven."

"Well, at any rate, there are ten of them. Beautiful ships, if you're partial to aircraft. Again: welcome aboard." The man waved a hand about loosely. He was wearing a black suit with tight trousers that tucked into high strapped boots, and a jacket with many buttons up the front and a short split tail. His shirt was blue, fringed with lace, and closed at the soft collar with a black string tie. The effect was of sartorial elegance, in an unpressed sort of way.

"I've come to find out about you," the man said, "and to answer your questions, if any; a fair exchange, you must admit."

"I'm Ves Romero," Ves said, "and this is the Countess Tatiana Petrovna Obrian. We are your welcome guests. What are dergs?"

"Little mindless beasts wearing flat tin helmets," the man said. "And that's about all we know, except that they kill people. Why, we haven't figured out yet."

The man sat down facing them. "My name is Colonel Burr, and I'm in charge of this expedition—which is on its way home now with all deliberate speed. You are, of course, welcome to come with us; any other choice would be unthinkable considering the circumstances. Did you enter this world through the Translator on the observation tower? Would you like a cold drink, or coffee or tea, perhaps?"

"Coffee," Tatiana Petrovna said. "I am very partial to coffee. With cream and sugar, and perhaps the slightest taste of cognac."

"My pleasure, Countess," Colonel Burr said. He pushed a small red button over one of the portholes and a steward came scurrying in, his footsteps muted on the red carpet. "Coffee, Wagner, and cognac. A rum toddy for me, and whatever this gentleman wishes."

The steward looked expectantly at Ves. "Hem," Ves said. "Er, coffee would be fine. Just coffee. With milk."

"Very good, sir," the steward said, and he padded from the lounge on silent feet. He appeared, Ves noted, to be wearing slippers.

"A tradition of the dirigible service," Colonel Burr said

before Ves had a chance to ask. "Felt slippers. Lessens the chance of a spark. Hydrogen is very flammable."

"Tell me," the countess said. "If you know about the Intertemporal Translator, then why did you destroy it?"

"To prevent the dergs from using it, of course," Colonel Burr explained.

"Do the dirigibles use helium now?" Ves asked.

"Afraid not," Colonel Burr said. "For a variety of reasons. It would require effort on the part of the Primes, which they're not willing to expend. That's the main one. The hydrogen does give us ten percent greater lift, and I assure you it's perfectly safe as long as you're not careless with bombs or blowtorches."

"You're Prime!" the countess yelled as the realization hit her. "Thank God!" She threw her arms around the little Colonel and kissed him on both cheeks. He didn't appear in the least embarrassed, but clearly enjoyed the demonstration.

"I do apologize," Colonel Burr said when the countess released him. "I thought you knew, of course, or I certainly would have mentioned it. The *Titanic* is a Prime ship. The name is their sort of humor. The ship's captain, Captain Herrington, and most of his officers are Prime. I myself, and most of my men, are expatriates, or refugees if you prefer."

"You're not any relation to Aaron Burr, are you?" Ves asked suspiciously.

"My dear sir, I am indeed a very close relation to Aaron Burr," the colonel said, "being the gentleman himself."

"Well," Ves said. "This is an honor, sir, a real honor." He shook Colonel Burr's hand firmly. "I've been searching for you."

"Do tell," Colonel Burr said cautiously. "And now you've found me. I trust you hold neither a warrant nor a subpoena, and I warn you I shall not be extradited."

"Neither," Ves said. "As far as I know, my interest in you is purely friendly. I have an interesting story to tell you, in return for some information you may be able to give me."

"I like stories," Burr said, settling down into his chair. "Commence!"

"Wait a second," Tatiana Petrovna said. "First of all, where are we, and how are we to get back to Prime?"

"We are floating in mid-air over *Terra Incognita*, which land in another world would be known as New Jersey. We return to Prime Time by flying to the congruence of certain magnetic lines of force, as I understand it, where our captain shall push a button or connect a lever or screw a knob and we shall be translated."

"Why are you here?" Ves asked.

"An expedition," Colonel Burr said. "Only not in the grim, serious terms in which we usually think of the word. More like a picnic for the Primes—they expected no trouble in this new land. It's in a sector, apparently, where they have the patterns of change very well mapped."

"What happened?" Ves asked.

Colonel Burr shook his head. "The dergs," he said. "They're about three feet high, and seem to have but slight individual intelligence, like ants. But they get their orders from somewhere—probably the tin helmets. They kill people. Perhaps they eat them, we don't know. We think they are not from this planet."

"If it happened here, will it happen elsewhere?" Ves asked. "I mean, on other time-lines?"

Burr shrugged. "There's no sign of it," he said. "On this time-line it's nineteen thirty-five, or thereabouts. If your time is past nineteen thirty-five, I guess you're safe. We'll have to research it, if the Primes let us."

"Isn't it in their interest?" Ves asked.

"You'd think so," Burr said. "But they'd find it easier to interdict the whole area. Very conservative about their time-lines, are the Primes."

The steward padded softly back into the room and distributed the drinks. Then he padded out again.

"Your health," Colonel Burr said, raising his glass formally. "And yours, Countess." He sipped. "And now that story you were about to tell me. . . ."

"Did you sign the Constitution of the United States?" Ves asked.

Burr looked at him strangely. "No, sir," he replied. "I was in New York at the time. The Constitution was drawn up and signed by the framers in Philadelphia. The document came down more strongly for a centralization of powers than I would have liked."

"*Would* you have signed it?" Ves asked.

"I wasn't asked," Burr snapped. But then he looked

thoughtful, holding his thumb alongside his nose and staring off into space for a while. "I would have changed it if I could," he said, "in some small detail. But I could have signed it as it stood, with honor and pride."

"You did, Colonel, you did," Ves told him.

"How's that?"

"In one of these alternate time-tracks, Aaron Burr signed the Constitution of the United States in the space that is otherwise filled by Alexander Hamilton."

"With no changes?" Burr asked. "I had so little influence? Ah, well. . . . Does Hamilton know? It would crush poor Alex's heart if he were to hear. How do you know?"

Ves told the full story of the exchanged Constitution, and the events that had resulted from that. Burr sipped his drink slowly, his eyes veiled by some secret thoughts; but Ves never doubted that he heard and weighed carefully every word. Burr was an excellent listener: there was no doubt but that he cared, and that he took every word as seriously as you did yourself. When you finished telling Burr about a problem, you felt relieved; he cared, he listened, he asked intelligent questions, and surely the problem was now halfway to being solved. Ves felt this very strongly as he talked to Colonel Burr; it was an aura the Colonel projected. Ves knew that it was projected because it was true.

Ves would not have imagined that telling his story would take very long, but under the impetus of Burr's skillful questions, an hour had passed before he had brought Burr up to date.

Burr spoke not a word for a long while after Ves had finished talking, but sat and stared out the port and sipped what was now his second rum toddy. Finally he shook his head sadly. "The implications are broad," he said, "and not altogether pleasant for me. It brings a complex pattern into view—I shall have to think on it."

"Any light you can shed on my problem would be appreciated," Ves said.

"Oh, yours," Burr said. "I presume you mean the theft of your Constitution. No problem there. Only a limited number of choices; the task will be sorting them out to the right one. Then, of course, there'll be the problem of recovering the document after we establish who has it. But I'm sure something will present itself."

Burr drummed his fingers on the small table by his chair. "No, it's not the actual theft which concerns me," he said. "It's the implications in their choice of objects, and what that may mean to Hamilton and me."

"I'm sorry," Ves said, "I don't think I understand."

"We're fetish objects, you realize," Burr said. "Because of our involvement with one of the major branch-points in their parallel worlds, the Primes treat Hamilton and me somewhere between honored guests and minor dieties. That's why Hamilton can set up his own little colony on an alternate world and maintain his network of informants on twenty others with no bitching from them. That's why I'm allowed free access to any of these exploration trips—even to the point of letting me head an occasional one so they can get some useful work out of what I'm going to do anyhow."

"Then this is what you do?" Ves asked.

"As often as possible," Burr said. "I also read a lot. Imagine having two hundred and fifty years of literature suddenly thrust at you. That alone should keep me busy for a while."

"I would imagine," Ves said.

"Have you read Charles Dickens?" Burr asked.

"Yes, of course."

"The Old Curiosity Shop, Great Expectations, Cowber Limited, Oliver Twist. . . . Have you read Lewis Carroll?"

"I have."

"My enthusiasms bore you?"

"Not at all. Two of my favorite authors."

"Yes. Imagine being born too early to have read either in your lifetime. Truly a tragedy. A true tragedy."

"I never thought of it that way before," Ves said.

"Certainly," Burr said. "Think of *Jabberwocky.* What would life be like without *Jabberwocky?* Or *Father William:*

> *You are old, said the youth, and your limbs*
> > *are unstable*
> *And your hands are incessantly shaking*
> *Yet you dance down the length of the dining room*
> > *table*
> *Without any crockery breaking."*

"I don't think I know that verse," Ves said.

"Alternate universe?" Burr asked. "You might have an entire alternate version of *Alice* to read. Think of that!

> *I'm sorry that bothers you, William said to*
> *his ward,*
> *I do it to pleasure my dates.*
> *When next I assay a gavotte on these boards,*
> *I'll endeavor to step on the plates."*

"I think I prefer the one I'm familiar with," Ves said. "It's the possibility of choice that makes it so interesting," Burr said. "But now I must get back to my duties, such as they are. Make yourselves comfortable in here. I'll have some food sent in. We must speak further when we arrive at Prime."

NINETEEN

Prime Time was a disappointment. Nate didn't know what he'd expected, but this wasn't it. The trouble was, it was so much like everyplace else. *Every*place else. It looked like you were standing in the middle of one of the big Thirties movie lots: Modern New York in one direction, ancient Rome in another; from out of the corner of your eye you saw a bit of old Tombstone, and with a turn of your head Nieuw Amsterdam. Except that the sets had gotten thoroughly mixed up. New York and Tombstone were intermixed with Rome and Nieuw Amsterdam. It should have been exciting. What made it disappointing was that somehow it *looked* like a set. Nate had the feeling that if he walked around to the back of the buildings, he'd see the braces holding them up.

The It was concealed in a large boulder that stood in a clearing in the uptown forest. Benjamin Franklin drove him up there in a chaise after breakfast, shook hands with him, wished him luck, told him to come back if he needed help, jotted down a design for a new leaf spring for the carriage he had invented on the ride up, then rode off. Nate threw the switch, and found himself in the middle of Central Park.

He was in a large roped-off area surrounded by a circle of posts about ten feet apart. Each post had a light fixture on top and a sign about halfway down, with two or three letters on it. The letters were in alphabetical order on the posts, going around toward the right. Beside each post was a small desk with a stool. A man wearing a blue uniform and a visored cap was sitting at the C-D-E desk. Two ducks, male mallards, were standing solemnly between the S-T and the U-V-W posts, staring at Nate.

After what seemed a long pause one of the ducks quacked briefly at the other and the two waddled off. The man said, "Go to your proper post, please. Have you filled out your customs declaration?"

Nate looked around. Except for the man and the retreating mallards, there was no other animate life in sight. So the man must be talking to him. "No," he said. "Which post is proper?" He thought briefly about an improper post.

"State your name, comma, family," the man said.

Nate thought about that for a moment. "Swift," he said finally.

"Proceed to the S-T post and fill out the form you find on the desk," the man told him. "Someone will be along presently to help you."

Nate proceeded and found a pad of forms on the desk.

CUSTOMS DECLARATION
Prime Time
TO BE FILLED OUT UPON ENTERING PRIME TIME. PLEASE PRINT. ALTERNATE LANGUAGE FORMS ARE AVAILABLE UPON REQUEST.

Name, Family   Given,   additional
Address   State
Country   Zone*   Sector*
Present Sectorality   Sectorality of Birth
MALE| | FEMALE| | OTHER| | (specify)
Sex

Purpose of visit (be brief)
Proposed length of stay

CIRCLE ANY OF THE FOLLOWING ITEMS IN
YOUR POSSESSION:
ADHESIVES ALCOHOL ANIMALS (living, scopic)
ANIMALS (skins, hides, bones) ART OBJECTS
CHEESE DRUGS/MEDICINES ELECTRICAL
BATTERIES EXPLOSIVES FIREARMS
FIRECRACKERS FIREWORKS FRUIT
JEWELRY LIBORIAN ATTITUDES MECHANICAL
DEVICES[1] MEDICAL INSTRUMENTS PESCULES
PLANTS (scopic) PLAYING CARDS PROSTHETIC
DEVICES OR ARTIFICIAL PARTS RADIOACTIVES
SEEDS SPRAY CANS SUGAR YEAST (packaged)
[1]wrist & pocket watches excepted
HAVE YOU ANY ITEMS FOR SALE OR BARTER?
yes | | no | |
HAVE YOU A PRIME BONDSMAN OR ASSURER?
yes | | no | |
HAVE YOU ANY PHYSICAL ANOMALIES?
yes | | no | |
HAVE YOU ANY MEDICAL ANOMALIES?
yes | | no | |
IF YES TO EITHER OF THE ABOVE, YOU MUST
FILL OUT A MEDICAL CHECK CARD AND KEEP
IT WITH YOU FOREVER
*if you cannot otherwise identify your zone or sector,
state the exact date, Gregorian, in your sector at this
moment.
WHEN THIS FORM IS COMPLETE, PASS IT TO THE
INSPECTOR AND ANSWER ANY QUESTIONS HE
MAY HAVE. BE POLITE. BE BRIEF.
WELCOME TO PRIME

Nate filled out the form as best he could. He was surprised to discover that he had none of the listed items
in his possession. The list made no sense to him, but what
customs list ever makes sense to anyone? Why is it easier
to import semi-automatic rifles into the United States
than canaries?

The man with the visored cap eventually came over to
Nate's post and took the form. "Welcome to Prime, sir,"
he said. "Have you any tobacco?"

"No," Nate said. "I don't smoke."

"Pity," the customs inspector said. "Have you ever been convicted of a major crime not involving moral turpitude?"

"Did you say *not* involving moral turpitude?" Nate asked.

"We don't give a damn about your morals here," the inspector said.

"Oh," Nate said.

"About your convictions," the inspector said.

"No, I have not."

"Right," the inspector said. "This purpose of visit: 'To recover Constitution'. Could you expand on that a bit?"

"It was stolen," Nate said. "I believe it is here on Prime—at Prime?—and I'm going to try to find it."

"By what process do you intend to recover this document?" the customs official asked. "By the way, exactly which constitution is it? Whose, I mean?"

"The Constitution of the United States of America," Nate said.

The inspector examined Nate's form and did some computation in the margin. "I see," he said. "The Constitution of the United States of America, Zone A-27, Sector 10."

"Is that where I'm from?" Nate asked. "Or do I mean 'when'?"

"I've made an arbitrary decision," the customs agent said. "That's what I'm paid for. Now: by what process do you intend to recover this document?"

Nate considered. "Sweet reason," he said finally. "Or, if that fails, I may make a monetary offer."

The customs officer considered that suspiciously for a long moment. "I don't see how that would violate our laws," he said. "You don't intend using any violence or threats of violence? You don't intend to attempt a theft of the document?"

"Of course not, sir," Nate said. "What sort of man do you take me for?"

"Humph," the customs agent said. "You may have a twenty-one day visa." He pulled at a corner of the desk which unhinged and opened, revealing a new writing surface and a row of rubber stamps: big stamps, small stamps, complex readjustable stamps, date stamps, time stamps, status stamps, authorizing stamps, rejecting stamps, undecided stamps. Pulling a card from a stack in one of many cubbyholes, he printed some words on it with his pen and then started using the stamps with something approaching abandon. Finally he handed the card to Nate. "Keep this with you at all times. If you wish to extend your visit past the twenty-one days, apply at any post office. I should tell you that if you get into any trouble here you are subject to immediate transtemptation without formal proceedings. Travel to Prime Time is a privilege, not a right."

"Transtemptation?"

"Work it out. You may go."

Nate wandered out of Central Park into a Roman-Dutch-Highrise section of town, wondering what to do next. As far as he could tell there were three things he had to accomplish: one: get hold of Ves, two: get hold of the Constitution (of the United States of America, Zone A-27, Sector 10), three: get home. But first things first; he must find a restaurant. A small, unpretentious. . . .

"Nate!"

He looked around.

"Nate, do you hear me?"

There was no one in sight. . . .

"Nate, this is Ves. Are you there? Do you hear me?"

The transmitter! "I'm here, Ves. Ves, where are you?"

"Nate, this is Ves, do you hear me?"

Nate found the button in his lapel and squeezed. "Ves! I'm here! I'm here!"

"Nate this is . . ." there was a clicking sound, then a pause. Then a woman's voice, with exceptionally fine diction, cut in. *"Mr. Swift? Will you please hold the line for a second, I'll be right with you."*

"Certainly," Nate said. Then: "Huh?"

TWENTY

|||||||||||||||||||||||||||||

The P.E.F.S. *Titanic* pulled up to one of the great mooring posts at its home base at Lakehurst, New Jersey,

Prime. Colonel Burr took Ves and the countess through customs and into the trolley to New York. "You'll need a place to stay," he said. "I recommend the *Great Auk and Gremlin* as a modest hostelry of moderate price, where the management still observes something of the old school of service."

"Modest price," Ves said. "What do we use for money?"

"Whatever you have," Burr told him. "As a matter of fact you can probably establish a line of credit with them. They can call up to verify your references."

"Call up?" Ves said, only mildly surprised.

"Certainly. There is an interchange Translator between Prime and most of the advanced sectors. It works as a vibrating column of air between two diaphragms. Sounds very hollow and distant, but it works fine."

"Very hollow, eh?" Ves said. "I suspect I've spoken to Prime myself on occasion. Shows you, one shouldn't blame the telephone company for everything."

"I, myself, can stay but overnight," Tatiana Petrovna said. "I must be getting back to Imperial Russia and my own time. I have obligations."

"Really, Countess?" Burr asked. "What a pity that you must leave. You will, of course, do me the honor of dining with me tonight. And you also, Mr. Romero."

"Delighted," the countess said, extending her hand, which Colonel Burr promptly kissed.

"I'd like to thank you for your help, Countess," Ves said, "I'd still be in prison but for your aid."

"I could not do less," the countess said. "In recognition of the historic friendship between our two countries. Mother Russia never forgets."

"Of course," Ves said. "But nevertheless, I feel I must thank you. I hope we may meet again."

"Undoubtedly," Tatiana Petrovna said. "The travelers between the times are a brave and hearty band. Once you are a member, it is hard to resist the lure of the It. We will meet again, at some unknown shore in some ancient time. . . ."

"You'll meet again for dinner tonight," Burr said. "Save the romantic farewell until you need it."

The trolley entered a tube-like tunnel, then the wheel-clack sound stopped and the trolley began swaying and bouncing. When it emerged from the tunnel a few seconds later it was about twenty feet above the ground, swaying gently, and the track had disappeared.

"What happened?" Ves asked, sticking his head out the window and trying to find what was holding them up.

"The trolley has switched from tracks to cables," Burr told him. "We cross over the Hudson on a pair of overhead cables. Saves the problem of having to build a bridge."

"Aha!" Ves said nervously, "very clever. Thick cables?"

"Haven't lost a trolley in months," Burr reassured him. He laughed at Ves's expression. "Welcome to New York, Prime," he said.

"New York Prime," Ves repeated. "Sounds like a cut of beef."

The trolley service terminated in a large trolley barn on the Manhattan side of the river. A variety of vehicles awaited them at the taxi exit to the barn: checker cabs, yellow cabs, hansom cabs, cabriolets, barouches, chariots, hackneys, victorias, a charabanc, a jinrikisha, and a dogcart. "Pick a conveyance," Burr said. "I will drop you at your hotel and continue on. Dinner in about four hours; that should give you enough time to relax and um—uh, you haven't any luggage, have you. Perhaps a bit of shopping."

"An impressive variety," Tatiana Petrovna said, "but I see no droshki."

"A serious oversight," Burr said. "I shall inform the town council."

They settled on one of the victorias, where they could sit comfortably facing each other. "Cultural shock," Ves said. "I feel a slight case of confusion at this mix of cultures. I mean, look at this block we're passing: a small Roman temple, a pair of brownstones, a Victorian manor house, and a glass-faced office building. And they all look new."

"Not new," Burr said, "just well cared for. The Primes take great stock in appearances. It doesn't matter *what* you look like, understand, but you'd best do it well. Let me tell you the trouble with this invention, the It. It's the last thing the Primes ever discovered. Now they import everything. They have no science of their own; they have no art of their own; they have no culture of their own; they import their laws with their food, their attitudes with their clothing. It's a completely amorphous society. It has no form of its own, it merely assumes disguises."

"What are *you* doing here, Colonel Burr?" Ves asked.

"They say I'm searching," Burr said.

"For what?"

"Some say I'm searching for my wife, some for my daughter, some for myself. I consider the last the most likely; but as far as I know myself, I am merely passing time and learning. I have some vague thoughts of teaching someone—I don't know who—after I've done learning. Not that one can ever be truly done learning unless one is also done with life—which I shall never willingly be. Here is your hotel."

Ves and the countess checked in and went to their separate rooms to their separate tasks. Ves, with credit established at the hotel—they accepted any credit card from anywhen—went on a small shopping spree. A double-edge razor, blades, a comb, underwear, overwear, upperwear and lowerwear. He tried to pick a suit as close to his own time style as he could find. He ended up looking like a gangster circa 1925, broad lapels, pin stripe and all.

"Elegant!" the countess declared, when he met her in the lobby.

"You take my breath away, Countess," Ves said, staring at her. A rose-red gown replaced the riding garb, and her chestnut hair was swept up and expertly tossed about on her head, topped with the simplest of diamond tiaras.

"You like it?" the countess asked, running her hands down the silken fabric covering the curve of her hips.

"Am I not a man, Countess?" Ves asked.

"You are very *gallant,* sir," the countess said, pronouncing it *á la Francaise.* "You think Colonel Burr, he will like it?"

"So that's it," Ves said. "I should have guessed. I've read about him. What does he have. . . . ? Countess, he will be enchanted, you have my word."

And so the Colonel was, when he came for them some ten minutes later. "Enchanting, Countess," he said, kissing her hand. "You have made good use of your time. And you, Mr. Romero, you look like a new man. An importer of Dutch chocolate I once knew, to be precise. Shall we go to dinner? I have reserved a booth for us at Delmonico's."

Over dinner they discussed many things. Colonel Burr possessed the ability to discourse brilliantly on any subject, as he proceeded to prove. The countess looked at him with increasing admiration after each course. Finally, when their flaming dessert was blown out and served, they got down to Ves's current problems and worries.

"Your friend will show up here in Prime," Burr said. "No need to worry about him."

"How will I find him when he does arrive?" Ves asked. "Put an ad in the papers?"

"One possibility," Burr said. "But why not use that transmitting device you mentioned? I assume he also carries one? You merely broadcast over it until he responds."

"Its range is very limited," Ves said. "A couple of blocks at most."

"So? Contact the City Paging Service. They broadcast messages for subscribers in this area. I'm sure they can duplicate the frequency of your transmitter. A wire loop with your voice on it can be broadcast periodically. Then they listen for your friend's reply, and direct him to your hotel. Simple?"

"I'll be in touch with them in the morning," Ves said.

"And now about this Constitution thing. These people here on Prime really have no regard for anyone else. It's amazing, their attitude. I think it must be a private collector or dealer; if it were a government, museum or other official project, I feel sure I should have heard of it. I've been carefully thinking that point over. And, I must admit, I made some inquiries this afternoon. Nothing official is happening along that line," Burr told Ves.

"And how do I go about finding this private collector?" Ves asked.

"I like your earlier suggestion," Burr said. "Advertise."

"Come to think of it," Ves said, "that's how I got here."

"You told me you were a private inquiry agent in your own time," Colonel Burr said. "I see no reason why whatever techniques worked successfully for you there would not be equally rewarding here."

"But I know so little about this time," Ves said.

"It's just like your own time," Burr said, "And mine, the countess's, ancient Rome, and any other period you can think of. That's the glory of it."

And so Ves went away after dinner, leaving Colonel
Burr and Countess Tatiana Petrovna still at the table,
staring into each other's eyes and holding hands. "No,
no, that's quite all right," he assured them as he left.
They may even have heard him.

The next morning Ves went to the offices of the City
Paging Service, who were delighted to be able to help him.
They made a wire loop of his voice—they used wire re-
corders instead of tape—and promised to broadcast it
every fifteen minutes, and listen for an answer for the
next ten. Then Ves settled down to work out a program
for locating the Constitution.

There were several possible approaches. An ad in the
appropriate paper might be the simplest. After all, the
present possessor of the Constitution had nothing to hide
here in Prime; the law was on his side. Crimes committed
in other time zones were not punishable or extradictable.
Interviews with dealers and collectors might be fruitful if
the possessor was reluctant to come forth. After all, such
desires grow upon a person gradually. The possessor's
colleagues might know of his desire, even if not aware
of his actual acquisition of the document. Both of these
approaches could be pursued simultaneously. What Ves
needed was a list of the names of collectors and dealers,
and the names of whatever periodicals they mostly read.
(Collectors of what? he wondered, dealers in what? Well,
that would sort itself out.)

Ves went to the city directory at the front desk of his
hotel to hunt up the name of an appropriate dealership in
his area to which he could go and ask questions. It wasn't
exactly a telephone directory, due to the peculiarities of the
Primes. Some of them had phones, others teletypes, others
visicables, others centcomp receptors. There seemed to be
no central company to service all of these competing forms
of communication. Indeed, there were at least three competing companies in Manhattan offering only telephone
service: Bell Telephone Company; Lower Manhattan District Signaling Company; and Pictaphone Corporation.
And their services, apparently, did not interconnect.

After some searching in the Business section of the
book, Ves found the line he'd been looking for: *PIPPINN
& CRIE. Documents, Stamps, Coins, all sectors, all times,
bought & sold. Highest Prices Guaranteed 141 Upper Wall*

Upper Wall, the room clerk assured Ves, was only minutes away from the hotel on foot. So Ves footed it into the street towards PIPPINN & CRIE.

Upper Wall Street was out of Dickens by way of Disney. A narrow, twisty street of small two-story shops, with the upper floor overhung, it looked too cute, too clean, too well-drawn to be real. Ves half expected to see little instruction signs by the doors: *D-ticket needed, may be purchased at booth in Queen Victorialand.* But the signs were very pragmatic and businesslike, although excessively neat and well-lettered.

141 Upper Wall had a wrought-iron signbar with a swinging, intricately scrolled PIPPINN & CRIE. wooden signboard hanging below. Inside, the store was dark wood paneling, a few cabinets and display cases, and a host of mottoes and slogans about the walls. Across from the door a sign said, *Ask! Could it hurt?* Below that, a framed verse, decorated with painted eagles and dramatic whirls:

> From there to here
> From then to now
> To make it clear
> To show us how.
>
> Sideways in Time
> We dip our oar
> Above we climb
> Beyond we soar.
>   —Seessel

"And how may Pippinn and Crie. help thee?" a gaunt man in a bright green waistcoat and cutaway asked, emerging from behind the counter. "Excuse the poor rhyme. It's actually pronounced 'cray', you know."

"No, I didn't," Ves said.

"It is," the man assured him. "Phoenician, I believe. Before my time, of course; although I did know Pippinn. The original Pippinn, that is, not his son; whom I also know, of course. He is the owner. The son, that is. I am the manager. Phipps. At your service."

"It's, ah, only some information I need," Ves said.

"We do our best to oblige, whatever your need," Phipps said. "What would you like to know?"

"I'm looking for a, ah, Constitution. You know, of the

United States. Trying to locate a, ah, specific, ah, Constitution."

"Certainly," Phipps said. "Which one?"

"Ah, a, ah, well, mine. That is the one from my time—sector—which was stolen."

"In what way is this Constitution different from all other constitutions?" Phipps asked patiently. "That is, how can we differentiate it?"

"Well," said Ves, who hadn't expected such a helpful reaction, "it was signed by Hamilton. Alexander Hamilton."

"Most of them were," Phipps said.

"The one that was left in its place," Ves said, "was signed by Burr. Aaron Burr. In place of Hamilton."

"I know," Phipps said, "Alexander Hamilton. So that's what happened to it."

"How's that?" Ves asked.

"I'll tell you who took your constitution," Phipps said. He reached behind him to the counter and flipped a magazine off the top, handing it to Ves. CURIOSITIES, VARIETIES, VARIANTS, it said across the top, THE INTERTEMPORAL COLLECTOR.

"The magazine?" Ves asked.

"Back page," Phipps said.

Ves turned The Intertemporal Collector over. The back page had an ad. Chitterly, Boatswain, Meloris, Pettiglob and Sims offered a whole page of documents and assorted intertemporal goodies for sale to the discerning collector. Like this:

23 Z9S29 Bill of Rights, 9 articles, (omit 7) sp $1,300
24 Z66S11 Capitulation of 1777 St. Fr.   gd $2,500
25 Z7S9 Annexation of Mexico—draft of Jefferson's
"   official speech before Congress (r) fr $3,500

"These people have our constitution?" Ves asked.

"One of them does," Phipps said. "Chitterly, by name. Now this is just a guess, but it's a pretty well-informed guess. Just don't use my name."

"Why do you think this man Chitterly has my, our, the Constitution?"

Phipps considered. For a moment Ves thought he wasn't going to tell, and so did Phipps. But then he nodded his head, his mind made up. "It's just an opinion, you know. But it makes sense. You see, Chitterly wasn't trying to steal your Constitution—the one with the Hamilton signature. He was trying to conceal the Burr Constitution."

"I'm afraid I don't follow that," Ves said.

"Señor Chitterly is what in polite society is referred to as a fence," Phipps said. "Not only that, but he has been suspected of committing the one unforgivable offense here in Prime: he steals from his friends. It's all right to purloin papers from the lower zones, but to steal here in Prime is a venal sin, sir. And of that is Chitterly suspected. The Burr Constitution is a valued relic that has been in a private collection since it was acquired some thirty years ago. Shortly after it was signed, you see, in its zone."

"And?"

"And it disappeared. Chitterly was suspected—never mind why—and a group of us went to beard the jackal in his den. The visit was a complete surprise and, by applying certain forms of moral persuasion, we were able to completely search the premises, including certain secure, secret sections. Several constitutions were found, but none had the Burr variation. One of the constitutions there was uncatalogued, and was undoubtedly yours."

"I think I see," Ves said.

"There was a tabletop It on his workbench. The old principle of the purloined letter—you're familiar with the purloined letter?—faked us out completely. We use the midget It to fish for valuable documents. It didn't occur to any of us that he might have hidden the Burr Constitution by running it through the It and geting your version in exchange; trading down, so to speak."

"How can you tell if that's true; if that *is* what he did?" Ves asked.

"Easily," Phipps told him. "Just run the Constitution through the It again. Since the Burr variant and yours changed once, they have the highest affinity and would reverse again."

"So why don't you go back and make the experiment?" Ves asked.

"Can't," Phipps said. "Caught him unawares the first time. Now he'll have applied to the magistrates for protection against a recurrence of our, eh, invasion. Law lets you get away with anything—almost anything—the first time. Now if we'd *caught* him . . ." Phipps sighed wistfully.

"How do you suggest I go about getting my constitution back?" Ves asked.

"Wait," Phipps said. "It might be a couple of years, or longer, until the heat dies down. But I'm sure he's got a customer for the Burr variant. He'll hang on to your version until the heat dies down, then he'll make the switch and you'll have yours back again."

"We can't wait a couple of years," Ves said. "Suppose I get another midget It and make the transfer with the Burr Constitution?"

"Then you'll get yet a third variant. The tuning is critical, and there's no way to duplicate his exactly, even if he would let us examine it."

Suitably disheartened, Ves returned to his hotel. Nate was sitting in the lobby waiting for him.

Ves did a double take, then yelled, "Nate!" and hugged his friend.

"Ves!" Nate replied, slapping Ves on the back. "It's good to see you. It's unbelievably good to see you. That's quite an answering service you set up here."

"When did you get here?" Ves asked. "Where've you been?"

"About half an hour ago," Nate said. "I've been . . . it's been . . . I have some stories to tell you. I have a feeling you'll believe them. You probably have some stories to tell me too."

"Over lunch, Nate, old friend, over lunch. And a bottle of Chianti. Have they Chianti? They must have! Come into the dining room, come!"

TWENTY-ONE

|||||||||||||||||||||||||||||||

Nate leaned back in the most overstuffed chair the *Great Auk and Gremlin* lounge had to offer and sipped at the first coffee he'd had since he left Ves's house, a lifetime before. Pretty decent coffee it was, too. "So now it's our turn to beard the vulture in his den, eh?" he said. "You've done a competent job, Ves. That's the 'in' phrase among us government service types this year, 'a competent job'. All understated and everything."

"Phipps called this Chitterly a jackal, not a vulture," Ves offered. "And thank you for the praise, but it was pure blind luck."

"Well, you know what they say about luck," Nate said, "it comes only to the prepared."

"Then we'd best prepare," Ves said, deciding he didn't care what the management thought, and stretching his feet out on the couch. "Because we're going to need a bit of luck. How do we entice this Chitterly to hand the Constitution over to us? What can we offer him?"

"A large sum of money?" Nate suggested. "We can go back for it. The President can get it out of the un-allocated fund."

"I'm given to understand that our money is useful here only in small amounts," Ves said.

"Hmmm," Nate said. Suddenly his face brightened. "We could invade!" he said.

"Invade?" Ves asked, alarmed.

"Oh, not a major invasion," Nate said. "Not like D-day, or anything. Just a minor commando raid. A couple of dozen troops. . . ."

"I'm sure the President wouldn't approve," Ves said. "Remember what happened over El Salvador. And we couldn't keep a thing like that from Congress."

"Even to retrieve the Constitution of the United States?" Nate asked. "No, I guess you're right. Besides, President Gosport isn't willing to admit that the thing's missing in the first place, so he'd never authorize anything like that. But then what?"

"What we need . . ." Ves suddenly got a funny look on his face and stared off into space.

"Ves! Ves! What's the matter? The lobster dinner? I told you . . ."

"Nate!"

"What?"

"We *do* have something he wants!"

"What?"

"Come along," Ves said, sitting up and putting his feet on the floor. "We're going to get our Constitution back. Our very own!"

The Chitterly mansion was huge, spacious, and well guarded. They had to pass through three checkpoints before getting to the main house. "Tell Mr. Chitterly we have something he wants" proved to be the magic words that carried them through. They had to submit to a weapons frisk at the second checkpoint, but since neither of them was heeled, it didn't matter.

"Well?" Chitterly said when they finally got through to him. "Well? My secretary says you won't speak to anyone else. I warn you, you'd best not be wasting my time. Best not." He was a tall, thin, angular man with glittering, bird-like eyes and a small mouth. What there was of his hair was shock-white and stood out from his head like a horseshoe-shaped halo.

"We had to see you, Mr. Chitterly, on a matter of some importance to both of us," Ves said. "You will find it interesting."

"You have something to sell?" Chitterly asked, his eyes darting from one to the other. "I might be interested if you have something to sell. I can't afford much for my little hobby, but if it's in my price range . . ."

"The Burr variation," Ves said. "Heard of it?"

"What's that? What's that?" Chitterly looked annoyed. "Did Thomerson, Phipps or one of that crowd put you up to this? I don't have the damned thing, and if I did, I certainly wouldn't admit it to the likes of you."

"You misunderstand, Mr. Chitterly," Nate said softly. "*We* have it."

"It sort of fell into our laps, you might say," Ves said. "There we were with this simple, ordinary version of the Constitution—you know, the one Alexander Hamilton signed—when all of a sudden we noticed that he didn't."

"Hamilton, that is," Ves offered. "*Burr* did."

"Imagine our surprise," Nate said.

Chitterly thought this over for a minute. "You boys want me to buy this Burr document from you," he said. "But that would be receiving stolen property. I couldn't do that."

"Not when it's stolen on this sector, anyway," Ves said.

"You're thinking," Nate said, "that all you have to do is stick that common old Hamilton document back in your little machine and *blip*, you'll have the Burr back, aren't you?"

"But it's not so," Ves said.

"We've altered it, you see," Nate said.

For the first time Chitterly looked startled.

"Wax," Ves told him. "In the pores and everything. We picked wax because it can be removed. But until it is, the Constitution weighs about three times what it should."

"Never transfer," Nate said. "Not a chance."

"I don't believe you," Chitterly said.

"Try it," Ves said, waving an airy hand at the tabletop It in the corner. "There are no witnesses. You can deny anything we say. Who'd believe us?"

"Who indeed?" Chitterly said. "*I* certainly don't."

"We just thought you'd be interested," Ves said, shrugging.

"There are others who would," Nate said. "Sorry to have bothered you. We won't be back."

"Wait!" Chitterly said. "Wait a second. As you say, there's no harm in testing your story." He hurried into another room and presently they heard sounds that might have been a vault door, or possibly a refrigerator opening and closing. Then he emerged with a rolled-up document.

"If it is as you say," Chitterly said, "this won't work. Then we can negotiate." He put the document in the basket of the It, set a dial, and flipped a switch.

The rolled-up document turned into a flat document. "Ha!" Chitterly said.

"Ho!" Nate said. "Is that the Burr Constitution?"

"Indeed, gentlemen," Chitterly said, peering at it. He looked up to see Nate and Ves advancing toward him. "So that's it," he cried, backing up rapidly. "Simple robbery! Well, you'll never get out of here alive."

"You misunderstand," Ves said. "We wish nothing from you."

"You have already given us what we came for," Nate told him.

"What? What's that?"

"The Constitution you just switched to get back the Burr Variant," Ves said. "It's ours. We wanted it back."

"Now we have it back," Nate said. "And we intend to keep it. He pushed the It off the table. It fell to the floor and shattered into fifty pieces.

Ves stomped on the pieces, feeling them turn to powder

satisfyingly under his foot. "We're done here now," he said. "Thank you for your time, Mr. Chitterly. We must be off."

TWENTY-TWO

|||||||||||||||||||||||||||||

Mrs. Montefugoni sniffed. "Wipe your feet, you come in here," she said.

"Is that the first thing you say to me. I've been gone for almost two weeks," Ves demanded, "wipe your feet?"

"You'd better do what she says," Nate said, following Ves into the room. "You're home now."

Mrs. Montefugoni brightened. "Good a see you, Commissioner," she said. "I go make coffee."

"Make enough for three," Ves said. "And some of your tartes, if available. We have a distinguished guest."

Smiling politically, the President of the United States came forward and extended his hand. "Mrs. Montefugoni," he said. "I've heard so much about you. Your two friends are heroes, do you know that? Heroes. Secret heroes, as it happens, but nonetheless heroes."

Mrs. Montefugoni sniffed. "Wipe your feet," she told the President.